THE EXECUTIONER OF YRECEP FOREST

First Edition published August 2023
Published by Indies United Publishing House, LLC

Cover art designed by YaYa Designs

ISBN: 978-1-64456-619-0 [Paperback]
ISBN: 978-1-64456-620-6 [Mobi]
ISBN: 978-1-64456-621-3 [EPub]
ISBN: 978-1-64456-622-0 [AudioBook]

Library of Congress Control Number: 2023938052

INDIES UNITED PUBLISHING HOUSE, LLC
P.O. BOX 3071
QUINCY, IL 62305-3071
INDIESUNITED.NET

The Executioner of Yrecess Forest

Laura DiNovis Berry

INDIES UNITED PUBLISHING HOUSE, LLC

Table of Contents

Chapter 1..1
Chapter 2..6
Chapter 3...15
Chapter 4...22
Chapter 5...32
Chapter 6...47
Chapter 7...53
Chapter 8...64
Chapter 9...74
Chapter 10..82
Chapter 11..90
Chapter 12..95
Chapter 13...102
Chapter 14...107
Chapter 15...113
Chapter 16...121
Chapter 17...128
Chapter 18...137
Chapter 19...144
Chapter 20...150

Chapter 1

The Brothers

Whispers rustled in the dark spaces behind the impenetrable, old trees. Anicen's arms ran with chills as he realized their black gnarled roots stretched out into the soft, honey yellow grasses as if they were reaching to grab his ankles and drag him into the forest. He took a step back, bumping into his little brother, Capar. The younger boy shoved him and whined, "Watch it, Anicen!"

Anicen wrinkled his nose at Capar before giving the thin rope in his hand a quick tug. Marjorie the goat bleated at him in return for his efforts. Her dark brown ears flapped against her curled horns as she tossed her head obstinately. Anicen tugged the rope again to pull the stubborn goat forward.

"Come on, girl!" he grunted. Capar rushed to the goat's side, wrapping his arms around her smelly neck.

"She doesn't want to go into the forest! And I don't either! It's scary!" he cried. Anicen loosened his hold and tried to relax his frightened heart. While he wouldn't admit it aloud, he didn't want to go into Yrecep Forest either. No one from his village ever entered the forest as far as he knew. A foreboding aura emanated from the branches of those black trees. Intuitively, Anicen knew to stay away, but the strange cries, and sometimes what he thought were human screams, that would tear through the branches also served as a strong warning to keep clear.

"Yrecep Forest is a dangerous place," his father would always say whenever Anicen would ask him why the trees were black or what the dark shapes moving between them were. The village hunters never even went close to that menacing forest, and if their prey happened to make its way through the treeline, they gave up the chase. There was nothing worth a trek into Yrecep Forest, or at least, there hadn't been until today. Anicen squared his shoulders and tried to look resolute.

"Capar, Ma told us to hide until it's safe. The Vuglar raiders could be at the village any time now. We have to go into the forest. It's the only way the Vuglar won't steal Marjorie... or us," he admonished. Capar only stared down at his leather-wrapped feet and clutched the goat harder. Anicen knew his brother would have much rather run off with the other village children and those too old to fight toward the big town, but Anicen had heard his parents whispering angrily. They argued back and forth about how best to keep their children safe.

Running to town for help would be a sound plan only if they had enough time to make the two day journey before the attack. But it was this morning, just after daybreak, that Rowar, one of the village hunters, had scrambled back up the hill and pounded on every door she passed, shouting, "The Vuglar are coming! Quickly, to arms! To arms!"

There was no time to make the journey safely. It was much more likely that after decimating the village, the Vuglar would rush after those escaping along the path through the open plains and carry them back to their mountain stronghold or cut them down where they stood. Anicen's mother and father had made their decision quickly. While a score of children and - grandparents fled toward town, they had rushed their children down the hill armed only with a small dagger, Marjorie the goat, and their burly yellow dog, Sweetness.

"The Vuglar won't follow yah into the trees. Yah'll be safe, my sons," their father had whispered into their ears as he clutched them to him before running back. Their mother gripped Anicen's chin and ordered, "Do not come out of the forest until yah hear our voices. Pa and I will come for yah."

Anicen could only nod, terror rendering him mute.

"Good boy," she had said. Then she too had turned and ran off to join her husband and the others as they made ready for the oncoming attack.

As terrifying as it was, on this day, Yrecep Forest seemed to be the safest place for the two boys. Anicen looked away from his brother and up the large hill they had descended a few minutes ago. At its peak, he could see the big thatched roof of the village elder's home, and he knew that behind it sat his little house of dried mud and hay where his mother had hung herbs from the ceiling and filled it with sweet smells just the day before.

He loved life in his little village. When the time for work would come, the villagers would sit outside their homes and sing with each other as they completed their daily tasks. As they used the long grasses of the plains to weave baskets and even hats, they would sing of the mysterious gods from the Long Ago who slept in the old Yrecep Forest at the bottom of the hill and of the frightening beasts who attended them. Anicen loved those haunting old songs, but Capar would laugh himself silly when the older villagers would break out into the playfully barbed ditties about their "lazy" cousins who had left the village to live in the big town.

"They can't hunt or plow in spring, but they've taught their cheeks to sing!" On this final verse, the singers would always whirl around and give their bottoms a mighty whack. Whenever a lazy cousin did return to the village for a visit, this ditty was always performed in their honor. No songs filled the air today though, only frenzied shouting. Anicen and Capar could not make out the words, but they could feel the fear that tainted each muffled cry. Sweetness' cold nose against his hand jolted Anicen back into the present. The dog licked his fingers gently, and Anicen tightened his gut. He pulled on Capar's dirty night shirt haphazardly tucked into his knee length pants.

"Come on, Capar," he urged. "Let's go. It'll be alright."

Capar sniffled and rubbed his snotty face against Marjorie's fur before looking up at the village one more time. Anicen waited for his brother to finish his silent goodbye. The boys and their animal companions turned away from their home on the hill and made their way into Yrecep Forest where the old gods slumbered. As they walked past the first row of trees, the air grew cold, and Sweetness' ears perked up at sounds the boys couldn't hear. The dog growled softly, but deeper and deeper into the forest they went.

Hours later, smoke rose from the village, and bodies were strewn about the ground. Thankfully, it hadn't been an entire Vuglar raiding party that had come to ransack and plunder but only a group of juveniles taking part in a coming-of-age rite. Those who lived and returned with spoils would be greeted with open arms as adults in their community. Although Vuglar raiders of any age were fearsome in battle, the villagers had been able to scramble together an admirable defense.

Young Vuglar faces were sealed in silent screams by crude wooden pikes they had fallen on after being unseated from their steeds, large mountain lumes. These four legged beasts were a formidable sight with their dusky fur and antlers that their riders would sharpen into dangerous points made all the better for goring their foes. Many of the villagers suffered such a fate and yet, while it was smoldering and bleeding, the village still stood, silhouetted by the descending sun. Its color matched the blood streaked across the dirty faces of Capar and Anicen's parents.

Down the hill they stumbled, panting and exhausted but relatively uninjured. They called out for their children with hoarse voices as soon as their feet touched the long grass just before the forest. They heard nothing. They cried louder and moved closer to the menacing trees. There was no sign of the boys, or the dog, or the goat.

Past the cruelly twisted roots and stinging branches, the parents limped, calling for their sons. They screamed and cried until the moon's glow transformed the trees' bark into mocking faces. Exhausted, the parents went home, but they came again the next day to search, and the next, and the next, and the next — until a year had groaned by, and the boys were declared lost to Yrecep Forest.

Chapter 2
The Murder

Gentle snores swelled throughout the small room. Delbon sighed and opened her eyes, although there wasn't very much to see in the dark. She frowned, finally admitting that her insomnia would be claiming yet another victory over what she had hoped would be a restful night. While she had promised herself a good amount of sleep, she was far too agitated to enter the land of dreams; her brain kept popping with ideas, unanswerable questions, and brilliant visions that examined all the potential variations of her future. There were so many possibilities and so many unknown elements. It was incredibly frightening and thrilling all at once.

She took a few deep breaths to try and quiet her mind, but the usually calming technique did nothing for her now. Propped up on her elbow, Delbon played with her lover's hair for a moment and began fantasizing about their plan. She and Evlor were almost ready to execute it. Admitting it to herself made her heart skip with excitement. Just a few more bits and pieces were necessary for the two of them to squirrel away before they could safely embark on their journey. She wondered what they would find out there in the wider world.

What dangers would they face? Would there be monsters and enemies she could never have even imagined? Thinking of all the things that could go wrong made her grind her teeth together unconsciously. When Delbon realized what she was doing, she quickly released her muscles and instead focused on what marvels could await them. What wonderful sights would their eyes take in? She could hardly wait to find out. She let out a pleasant exhale of relief and laid back down on the bed. She curled up to her lover's back; the heat of the other body melted into hers.

With closed eyes, she tried to drift off into the pleasant dark. Yet as the minutes crawled by, sleep did not come. Delbon pursed her lips and opened her eyes again. Yawning, she decided it was no good to try and fall back asleep. While she appreciated that her mind was capable of quickly working when it came to constructing strategies and resolving difficulties she encountered, convincing herself to stop deliberating the worthiness of a scheme or how to solve potential problems so she could get some rest was not always an easy task.

She slipped out from under the thin blanket that kept her and Evlor snug. The small room was not too cold, but Delbon quickly put on her clothes. She used a thin leather strap to tie back her tousled hair before returning to the bed. She gave Evlor a gentle kiss on the cheek and rubbed the tip of her nose against the sleeping woman's neck, breathing in her scent. A wave of adoration flowed through her as she looked down at Evlor, deeply enveloped in her slumber.

"Soon," thought Delbon as she tucked the woman in, *"Soon, we'll be able to go wherever we want."*

Although her joy was radiant and singing within her, she left the room as quietly as a shadow, a large spear in her hand. If she couldn't sleep, she may as well try to acquire a few of those missing elements now. They would need food, water, and items for trade when they ran out of their supplies, and while they had managed to store up a good amount of provisions, they needed just a bit more to satisfy Delbon, who would much rather be safe than sorry. Despite the darkness that surrounded her, she broke into a large grin. Soon the pair of them would be far away and safe from this place of constant worry. They would be able to live out their days together peacefully as two old, grumbly fools. Yes, she would go out hunting now, and hopefully she would have the good fortune to obtain all they needed in one fell swoop. Then they would be prepared to set out for whatever adventures or dangers awaited them.

A few hours later, Delbon was huffing at a stray dandelion yellow curl that had fallen between her eyes. It fluttered tantalizingly, and Delbon thought, for a smug, divine second, that she had won the battle, but the curl settled back into place. More than a little irritated, she blew at it again. She shook her head. She even whipped it back and forth, but still it was no use. The curl sat squarely between her eyes, defiant.

She grumbled to herself as she went cross-eyed staring at the offending curl before letting loose a yawn so massive the bones in her jaw clicked as it slightly unhinged. As tiring as her late night excursion had been, it had, much to her satisfaction, proven highly successful. Now here she was, up to her elbows in an aseloni she had killed in the dark hours of the morning, hard at work removing the creature's internal organs. Her brain danced with the realization that after harvesting this beast, her preparations would be complete. She whispered a gentle chant of gratitude to the dead creature, thanking it for all its body provided her even though it was taken, not given. She promised she would not let the blood debt go unpaid and noted to herself that she would leave a gift for the rest of the aselonies.

The dead aseloni currently being gutted certainly did provide much security for Delbon. She could skin the beast for its hide, which would no doubt make for valuable trading material, and she could harvest the delicious meat. That she could cure, and it would become excellent food to eat while traveling. The slimy guts that wriggled under her fingers also had their uses. She knew of several individuals who would use the hardy aseloni bladders as containers for their magical potions, and the intestines and bones often were used as ingredients to make such mysterious concoctions. She was sure the bones too could be traded if she decided to hold on to them. She was well aware they could be sharpened into knives or carved into jewelry and little trinkets. With this kill, Delbon was certain that she and her lover would finally be ready to start their trek into the unknown.

Of course, while every inch of the aseloni was valuable, the prospect of getting bits of the dead beast in her hair was not appealing so she supposed that the stubborn curl would be staying where it was. Just as she had accepted her fate, a delicate finger entered her vision and gently moved the hair to rejoin its wild comrades. Delbon blinked in surprise at the newcomer.

Had she been so caught up in her thoughts that she had been completely unaware of this young woman's approach? Her teeth ground together. No, that couldn't be right. It was so quiet out here, and she hadn't been that consumed in thought. Delbon was perturbed. How had she been caught so off guard? Fall leaves were strewn everywhere. These generally served as a gentle alarm when crushed underfoot, and yet another person had been able to sneak up so close to her without her noticing. *How?*

A chill ran through Delbon's skin, but she shook it off as she watched her new companion yawn and stretch her back. Then she crouched down, eyes closed, face aimed into a fragile sunbeam. The sight struck Delbon as a picture of serenity, not of danger. Although her gut was twisting with a thousand frantic snakes, Delbon forced a thankful smile and raised her knife-wielding hand in greeting. The tender golden glow of the early morning sun glinted against the bloody stone blade. Dew still covered the ground. The air was calm. No, she thought, she would not make trouble where there wasn't any brewing. It would be best to keep this interaction as friendly as possible until it was over, and then she could carry on with her plans.

"It's odd to see you here. I thought you hated guttings," Delbon remarked, her voice warm despite the coolness in the air. Her quiet companion smiled a little and shrugged before taking a deep drink from a waterskin that hung from her shoulder. Delbon's eyes brightened as she licked her lips. She hadn't had anything to eat or drink for quite a bit, and while her body had let her deprive it for a time, the sight of nourishment suddenly made her mouth dry with jealousy. She watched the young woman swallow, ascertaining that this wasn't some performance for her benefit, that the young woman had in fact ingested the liquid before she said, "Oh, I'm parched! Share some of that with me?" The young woman cocked an eyebrow, but she nodded and held out the waterskin. Delbon waggled her dirty hands.

"Maybe you'd better pour it for me," she suggested. Without hesitation, the young woman moved closer to pour the water into Delbon's open mouth. Delbon swallowed and bobbed her head to indicate her thirst was sated. She smiled.

"Thanks for that! This one's a big ol' -" Delbon jerked suddenly and began to retch. Her fern green eyes, usually so easy for others to get lost in, swelled in her head as her bloody hands clawed at her throat. She continued retching as a yellow foam bubbled from between her lips. She sputtered in disgust. A horrible fire was burning within her belly. It sent searing shock waves of pain throughout her gut.

"Poison," Delbon thought. *"She's poisoned me. Vomit. Vomit NOW."* She dropped her knife and gripped her hands together before slamming them into her stomach, over and over. Her companion sat, patiently waiting for her to finish, and then commented, "It's too late. You're already dead."

Rage and panic erupted within Delbon. She couldn't die now; she was so close to getting out, to accomplishing her goal. She staggered to her feet, desperately trying to breathe. When she saw the smile on the young woman's face, she wanted to scream in fury, but the only sound that came from her throat was a revolting gurgle. It was soon followed by yellow bile mixed with her blood. Ignoring the destruction of her internal organs, she leaned down to grab the knife.

"You'll die with me then," Delbon snarled in her mind, clutching the knife as if it were a lifeline. She lurched towards her assailant, yearning to cut her open from neck to navel, to slice this abhorrent beast up just as she had done to the aseloni. It would be a righteous kill. Delbon wanted to see the young woman's guts ravaged just as she knew hers were being ravaged. Despite the sudden onslaught of rage, despair overcame her and flooded her spirit. All of her plans, all of her dreams — robbed in an instant. Her body was already too weak to fight; she fell to her knees. Her hand dropped the knife.

Delbon knew then that everything was coming to a close. She cradled herself during her final moments, remembering her lover's face and the warmth of that tender cheek as she kissed it before leaving their cozy sanctuary. It felt at once like it had happened both a lifetime and mere seconds ago. Her mind sent her back to that sweet place, and she lowered herself onto her bed. Now safely tucked under the blanket, she cuddled closer to her lover. Her arms slipped around the other woman and held her close. They could leave tomorrow. Today, they would stay in bed, safe and warm. With those happy images flooding her sight, Delbon surrendered.

With one last violent bout of retching, she collapsed to her side, dead at last. Her murderer moved to all fours to survey the expression that was frozen onto her death mask; it was one of resigned dismay.

"Thank you for your sacrifice," the murderer half giggled as she leered at Delbon. A ray of sunshine turned the tears that had welled up in her eyes into delicate crystals, and her eyes themselves glittered like precious jewels. It was as if the sun, distressed at Delbon's horrific end, had transformed her body into a work of art to be cherished for all eternity.

The murderer did not seem to notice. She had no time for

art. She had work to do, and so she withdrew a clay jar and a long bone hook from her robe. She wiggled the cork stopper out of the jar. Once the cork was removed, she began inserting the long hook up Delbon's nose. Bits of that once magnificently energetic brain, still pink with blood, saw the world in a way it was never supposed to before being dropped into darkness that came not from the protection of a skull but from an uncaring clay jar. Humming, the murderer inserted the hook a few more times, filling the jar almost to the brim before popping the cork back into place.

With no apparent feelings of guilt for what she had just done, the murderer stood and left the two carcasses behind. Delbon's body lay next to her catch as her now frozen face stared at the brilliant sky, where clouds drifted to faraway realms she had often dreamed of but would never get the chance to see. That defiant curl fell back between her eyes as the yellow bile began to harden on her still lips.

Within minutes, shadows covered her face as six figures dressed in robes surrounded her. They stared down in grim silence as one fell to the ground and began to wail, "My child, my child!"

Another knelt to console the sobbing wretch.

"Hush, Efil, hush."

Ignoring the cries, one of the group said, "She is becoming a threat."

"Perhaps, Yerif," a second responded. The rest said nothing; they only stared down at Delbon's once mesmerizing eyes.

"Perhaps? How can you say that, Divorc? We've never seen such depravity!" hissed Yerif. Another voice piped up, "We don't know her reasons for doing this, but it is upsetting the balance."

Divorc looked between Yerif and this new speaker, sour at these protests.

"Regardless, Koa, a sacrifice is always to be honored, and

so we must prepare Delbon's body. Arni, go wake up the others. We'll be ready by the time they've arrived."

"We can't accept this!" Yerif protested.

"We must! As it is in nature, so it will be with us!" Snapped Divorc. "Even rabid beasts are put out of their misery," retorted Yerif through bared teeth. "Let us honor Delbon and then destroy-"

"-Arni. Go."

Arni nodded curtly and left per Divorc's instructions. A frosty silence shrouded the group.

"Whatever foul sickness comes because of this... let it be on your head," growled Yerif, glaring at Divorc with a face of poison. Divorc said nothing and bent down.

"Let go of her, Efil," Divorc ordered. Efil had drawn Delbon close and clutched her, refusing to let go.

"She doesn't deserve a blessing from Delbon!" Efil howled. "Yerif is right! She's gone rabid! Kill her! We must ki-"

Divorc drew back a fist and punched Efil in the face. Efil fell back, shocked.

"Get a hold of yourself! What we must do is prepare her body," Divorc snapped before looking around at the remaining figures with disgust.

"Well, help me!" she said as she grabbed Delbon's ankles. The rest, including Yerif, joined in, and together, they lifted Delbon's body into the air. Efil followed with tears marking a heartbroken trail. As the group disappeared with the corpse, Efil paused. Echoes of Arni's voice were ringing out, breaking the chilly quiet of the day.

"Awaken, coven! Awaken and arise for the Ritual. There has been a death, and we must pay homage!"

Sleepy grumbles met the announcement, and many people, some more anxious than others, began to look around their rooms to ascertain if it had been any of their companions who had been stolen during the night. As more and more of the coven awoke, names were called out, and friends sighed in relief when they heard a shout in response. Soon a large crowd had gathered. As Arni continued to call, "Join us so that we may honor the dead!", they moved as one to witness the Ritual and pay homage to whoever it was who had been killed.

Chapter 3
The Ritual

Birdsong trickled through small breaks in the tree branch woven ceiling. A thin trail of sunlight shone directly onto Pesdari's face as more of her coven milled about her. She had been woken early by the coven's call to gather here, and sleep still clung to her. She closed her eyes, refusing to move even as unknown shoulders bumped and buffeted against her. Her chin tilted upwards so she could drink in the sunlight. There was always a chill in the Hall that seemed to creep up from the packed dirt floor through her feet and into her bones. The intertwined trees that banded together to form the walls around the group of wild-haired children, gangly younglings, and wary younger adults stretched out their long, twisted branches to construct a type of natural roof above them as well. These branches were wound so tightly together that only a scarce amount of warmth could sneak through. This place seemed to clutch greedily at the damp cold of early morning and keep it in place all day long. The small kiss of sunshine on Pesdari's face was a rare gift. She let her head roll to the side with a gentle exhale just before a woman's voice overpowered the singing of the birds.

"I speak to all of you now with words the old gods have no use for. Mages, those cheap conjurers, are so far removed from the wellspring of power they call upon. They must use language as a crude hook so they may drag out but a trace of this natural gift. They can only muster a pittance of magic because they have forgotten how to properly worship the old gods. Well, we will honor them now, and through them, our gifts will grow."

Pesdari opened her eyes then with a rueful little huff. She always thought it was a bit funny that mages were derided so often by the coven leaders, especially since she only knew of one or two members of the coven who had actually ever met one, but, without fail, no matter the magical lesson of the day, the danger of sharing the coven's magical secrets with "foul minded mages" was pounded into everyone's head over and over. Stifling a yawn, she blinked herself back into the present.

Several yards in front of her was a woman, Divorc, the leader of the coven's rituals. She stood on a raised mound of earth that had its top flattened into a smooth surface over years of use. Two small steps carved into its side led to the floor. Divorc lifted her arms out wide; her fingers splayed apart. Her black robe hung off her wiry frame, and her neck curled back so the group before her could only see her bare throat and chin pointed to the roof. As Pesdari surveyed Divorc, she was reminded of a black-feathered bird sailing through the air.

"Egal, ruler of wind and air, must be given breath. Riefon, ruler of fire, must be given fuel. Tewar, ruler of water, must be given blood. Hetra, ruler of earth, must be given flesh."

As Divorc finished speaking, the large coven began to shift. Pesdari balefully watched as the crowd made way for five people, the other leaders of the coven, who had just entered the Hall. They were also wearing long robes but each was dressed in a different color. Pesdari continued to watch as they pulled something behind them.

Whispers of "*Who is it?*" "*Who did it?*" flittered all around her. She peered over a small boy's head and saw the prize the leaders hauled. Dragging through the dirt was the corpse of a young woman, no more than nineteen years old. She was wrapped in brilliantly white cloth from head to toe with only her face exposed. The five leaders moaned low, soft tones as they pulled the corpse along. Someone then screamed, "Delbon!"

Pesdari watched, intrigued, as a flash of dark brown hair whipped by her, its owner, a young woman stricken with a fate she could not yet accept was pushing surprised onlookers out of her way. She paused for just a moment, tears streaming down her face. A voice in the crowd hissed, "Evlor! Don't!"

Evlor didn't listen.

"Delbon!" she cried again launching herself at the corpse. Pesdari watched as one of the procession, Rouble, whipped around. In an instant, her hand dropped the rope and thrust out to catch Evlor by the neck. She employed the momentum of Evlor's flight to slam her hard onto the dirt floor. Pesdari could hear Evlor's sharp gasp as the air was cruelly knocked from her lungs. Rouble had a deep scar that cut across her shaved skull, but her most interesting feature at the moment was her hand. It no longer looked like flesh but stone as it held the wheezing Evlor in place. Some in the crowd jeered and whooped as Evlor gasped like a dying fish. Rouble did not move. Her jaw was set tight, but no true display of emotion contorted her strong face.

"SILENCE!" Divorc boomed. Her naturally reedy voice was amplified by sudden winds that whipped through the coven, and the intensity of it caused many to grip their ears in pain. A hush rapidly fell over the assembly. It was then that Rouble decided to remove her stone hand and push a heavy breath from her lungs. As she did so, thin fissures formed along her wrist and ran up each of her fingers. Little stony scales began to break off, revealing flesh underneath. More fell until her hand was of blood and bone once again.

"Our weak empower the strong," Divorc declared, her voice returned to its normal state.

"As it is in nature, so it is with us. Only the strong in mind and body can live long lives of power. Those of us who cannot feast become food. Those who are sacrificed feed into the source of our magic. Their lives were not in vain, and their deaths are not wasted."

Divorc's eyes rested on Evlor, who had scrambled to her feet and was held up by a few helpful hands. Divorc pointed a thin, pale finger at the stricken young woman. "We will *not* dishonor them with pitiful histrionics," she intoned. Evlor looked like she was going to rush forward yet again, but hands squeezed her shoulders and kept her in place.

The Hall soon filled with mutterings of agreement as Evlor was pulled back into the body of the coven. Rouble resumed her place, and the leaders once again began dragging Delbon's lifeless husk toward Divorc. As they got closer to the austere woman, the low tones of their chanting grew more frenetic and higher in pitch. They placed the corpse horizontally a few feet from Divorc before forming a line between their ritual leader and the sacrifice. They stood still, their wide eyes and bared teeth facing the crowd. Divorc waited for all the coven leaders to find their place in the line before commanding, "You who have provided this sacrifice of life and magic, come forward."

She who had provided the sacrifice made her way through the crowd. There were shocked gasps and disturbed mutterings as she did so. Pesdari heard someone scoff, "Thade? Again? She'll kill us all before winter."

Thade stood with her back to the group; her sable hair hung in a long braid against her ivory neck. She didn't pay attention to any of the murmurs around her and kept her eyes fixed on Divorc who said, "We thank you, Thade, for this gift of life. We thank Delbon from whom it was taken. Her sacrifice continues the flow of magic into our veins."

Thade replied, her voice light and beautiful, "I thank Delbon for her sacrifice and beg the gods for their blessing."

"Lower your robe and open your heart to the gods."

At this, the five leaders joined hands, forming a line of flesh. Thade, in turn, slipped her arms out of the sleeves of her robe and knotted them around her waist. Above them all, Divorc removed a glinting knife from the folds of her robes. She held it aloft with her left hand.

Closing her bulging eyes, sharp whistles cut through her teeth. She raised her right hand to her chest, all the fingers curled except for the fifth which stuck out into the air. With a hiss, she severed it at the first knuckle. The extremity fell into a wooden bowl at her feet. She stiffened only a moment before picking up the bowl. She puffed up her cheeks and blew into it, transforming her piece of finger into a thick mixture of blood, ground-up bone, and bits of flesh. Air bubbles rested on the top of the bloody concoction.

She carried the bowl to each leader, dabbing the mixture onto their waiting tongues. Then she went to Thade. As she did with the coven leaders, Divorc silently lined Thade's tongue before she dipped her finger back into the mixture. Then she drew a circle a few inches below Thade's collar bone and said, "Life and death, the endless circle, is in everything. As it is in nature, as it is with the gods, let it be so with you."

Thade responded solemnly, "As it is in nature, as it is with the gods, it shall be so within me."

Divorc, her little finger still dribbling blood, nodded before she walked away from Thade. She stopped just to the side of the line of leaders.

"Then, Thade, offer your sacrifice, and may you receive gifts in return from the gods!" she cried.

The two leaders on either end of the line aimed their open palms toward Thade. All five raised their voices to meet in one sonorous note as their backs began to arch. Pesdari's pulse quickened and she, along with many others of the coven, began to howl and sing. A strange, wild harmony swept through the Hall. The Song of Sacrifice rose through all their throats and pounded in their blood like wolves through snow.

Pesdari saw red orbs streaked with a yellow light flare-up in the palms of the two leaders on the ends of the little ensemble. The leaders all began to shake, and a bright light glowed at the back of their throats. Thade stretched her own arms out wide.

"We offer Delbon to Egal, to Riefon, to Hetra, and to Tewar!" shouted Divorc above the whirling song. "Gods! Accept this sacrifice, and give blessings to your student!"

Fiery, pulsating beams shot out from the two leaders' palms straight into the circle on Thade's chest. The entire group in the Hall was releasing wild cries, but Thade's piercing screams cut through the cacophony of song and howls. Her flesh sizzled and boiled underneath the powerful ray. Her eyes and fingertips glowed with a white fury. The beams disappeared within her chest, and the light once emitted by the leaders immediately vanished. All five of them began to drop to their knees or collapse to the ground, but Thade stood tall — now a pillar of radiant light and horrible shrieks.

The Hall went silent as she struggled to control the massive amount of magic rioting throughout her being and making her heart beat with a frantic madness. Panting, the leaders watched her. The audience in the Hall twitched with violent anticipation as a minute that felt more like an hour crept by. At last, Thade stopped screaming. The light once emanating from her entire being surrendered to a soft glow within her heart that was still strong enough to be seen through the skin on her back and front. She slowly moved her arms so that her palms pointed at the corpse on the ground.

"Accept my gift!" she cried, but her voice was not her own. It was simultaneously a brittle hiss and flaming roar that deafened the Hall. The coven seemed to flinch in unison at the power she held. The beam that had just penetrated Thade's chest was now expelled from her hands and fired at the waiting corpse. Wild undulations danced across moans and chants as the white fabric wrapping Delbon's lifeless body began to burn.

As it did, Delbon's eyelids flicked back. Her mouth dropped open. A long howl clawed out as flames danced along the fabric no longer white but now a deep garnet. Blood seeped through the wrappings and pooled onto the ground. Within seconds, the entire corpse was set alight. The flames were magnificent. The coven stamped their feet and raised their arms with triumphant, bloody lust as Delbon's body turned to dust under the flames. It was over in almost an instant. The flames did not die down slowly as they would have at a cooking fire but rather vanished entirely. Delbon's corpse disappeared along with the flames. Only a dark scorch mark indicated that the Ritual had been held at all. This absolute removal of the sacrifice meant that the gods were satisfied with Thade's offering and that the Ritual was complete. Thade collapsed to her knees.

All those in attendance looked around at each other with the dazed look of sleepwalkers interrupted. As the blood lust drained from their eyes, Pesdari noticed the exhausted pallor that always appeared in the Ritual's aftermath creeping onto their faces. The coven wandered off together like a tired herd of old beasts. A few crying little children found their hands gently taken by older compatriots as the Hall began to empty, but Thade remained on her knees, shaking and sweating. The exhausted coven leaders walked past her with no offers of comfort. Efil stared straight ahead with stony eyes, but Divorc, whose finger had already stopped bleeding, cast Thade a quick, wary glance before following the other leaders out.

Chapter 4
The Vision

While the Rite was always witnessed by the whole coven, actually communing with the old golds was a private matter, and the recovery from such an exhausting feat was typically done alone. There was little anyone could do really; it was a sacrament none but the parties involved could penetrate. Pesdari waited until all the leaders were out of the Hall — and out of earshot. When the last gentle thud of footsteps finally disappeared, she approached Thade. She raised a foot bound in a leaf woven slipper and gave Thade's left shoulder a soft kick from behind, leaving a dirt mark.

Thade didn't even glance back.

"Leave... me... alone," she panted. Pesdari kicked her harder in response. Thade grunted and nearly fell over. She righted herself before glaring at Pesdari. She was about to say something, but Pesdari interrupted her.

"Delbon's death was gratuitous. She never threatened you."

A sigh met the accusation.

"You know the blessing is immense if you offer a well-practiced magic user, Pesdari."

"Yes, but there's also unnecessary loss. Evlor loved Delbon."

"Pest," Thade began wearily, "Why would I waste my strength to spare a heart? Love is a risk in this place."

Pesdari ignored the use of Thade's annoying pet name for her and continued, "Delbon was powerful enough to get out. She could have left-"

"-But she didn't." Thade snapped. Her teardrop shaped eyes were narrowed, and while they were already near black in color, her eyes were made even darker by her foul mood.

"And why Iswe, Gaer, and Titber? Why so many, Thade? Why-"

"-If they had been stronger," Thade cut in, "If Delbon had been smarter... then she could have left this place and taken her precious Evlor. They *all* could have left! But I was the better of them, and I killed them. I deserve those blessings."

She gritted her teeth together. Her jaws tightened as she snarled, "I <u>earned</u> them."

Pesdari raised her eyebrows at the violence in Thade's expression. Then she realized that the outburst had used up the last of Thade's reserves. Exhausted tears streaked her cheeks, and haggard breaths wracked her lungs. Pesdari said nothing; she squatted down beside the other young woman whom she had known since childhood, and the two waited in silence for a moment.

"Evlor will come for you," Pesdari finally said. Thade closed her eyes; her demeanor returned to a placid state.

"Let her try," she replied, her voice cool. "You must have been cooking something new in order to get Delbon. She wouldn't have fallen for any of your usual tricks. What was it? What did you use on her?" questioned Pesdari. Thade rubbed her temples.

"Stop talking."

"What did you use?"

"You really do live up to your name, Pest."

"Tell me."

"Stop, or I'll kill you next."

"Not if I sacrifice you first. There would be no loss then."

Thade stretched her neck, unconcerned by Pesdari's threat.

"Oh, you'd miss me, Pest. I'm your only friend," Thade countered.

"No, I wouldn't. I would only remember you."

Thade met Pesdari's stony gaze and held it as if she were searching for any kind of warmth or reassurance. She found none, but before she allowed any evidence of hurt to show on her face, she used Pesdari's shoulder to push herself to her feet.

Pesdari grunted with annoyance, knowing her clothing would now be marked with blood. She stood as well and roughly popped her shoulder under Thade's armpit. Thade squawked at the indelicate treatment, but all the same, she smiled with weary gratitude as Pesdari wrapped an arm around her waist. No matter how Thade aggravated her, it was true. Thade was Pesdari's only friend, and while Pesdari could at times be called aloof and typically self-serving, she was not completely heartless. She was no stranger to the intense physical toll of the Ritual; just last month, she had made an offering to the gods herself.

An overambitious youngling, Vebra, who had been practically vibrating with raw talent, had tried to suffocate Pesdari by stealing all the air from her lungs. He would have become a true force of nature if he had only learned patience. While he did manage to wait until Pesdari had fallen asleep in her chamber, he had made a fatal mistake. He was not practiced enough in the magic of Egal to conduct his plan from a distance. To execute his attack, he needed to be close to Pesdari, so close that he would be able to coax out the air that was floating happily within her and invite it into his own body. So he had crept into Pesdari's chamber as she slumbered. His step had been light, but the pounding of his heart had been so loud, he had feared the whole coven would hear it.

But no one had heard him or sensed his murderous intent. He had reached Pesdari's bedside undetected and knelt down beside her. Gently, he proceeded to blow his own air supply over her nose and lips as an invitation to the element within.

Still asleep, Pesdari's lungs grew swollen as the magic infused gusts were inhaled. The lungs paused, still bloated with enchanted air, before completely emptying themselves. Vebra then sucked all the escaping air greedily in. Only then had Pesdari's eyes shot open with panic. Dry gagging noises hiccuped from her, and she had turned on her earthen bed to see Vebra scooting away from her towards the door. His hands were clasped over his nose and mouth so none of Pesdari's air could escape him. She had pushed herself into a sitting position and lunged at him but had fallen, gasping, to the floor.

Vebra had jumped then and moved toward the door of her chamber. Pesdari's arms reached out as if trying to catch him in an embrace. Just as he was about to back out of the doorway, Pesdari curled her hands into fists and slammed them together. Two large stones had flown out of the dirt walls on either side of the door. And there it was. Vebra's fatal mistake. He may have waited for Pesdari to fall asleep, but Vebra was not stalking simple prey. He was hunting a predator, one that could set traps. Before he even had a chance to know what was happening, Vebra's skull was crushed. As soon as his body fell, his magic was ended. Pesdari had frantically taken in a huge breath of air, staring at the bloodied attacker. When she could stand, she fetched the coven leaders to prepare what was left of Vebra's corpse for the Ritual. The following morning, Pesdari stood before the coven and made her offering as the screams and howls of the coven clamored behind her as she erupted into magic and pain.

And so, Pesdari knew that Thade would barely be able to cross the threshold of the Hall on her own. The enclosure, while it was immense in its height, did not possess the same grandeur in length. Under normal circumstances, a person could cover the entire threshold in mere seconds, but offering a sacrifice brought as much agony as it did reward. The pain that came with the Ritual still lingered in Pesdari's mind. The scalded palms and blistered chest had been excruciating, and she remembered collapsing face first onto the dirt floor, releasing agonized cries. Just as they had today, all the coven and its leaders had left without a second thought. Only Thade had stayed behind, and she had rolled Pesdari onto her back to alleviate the pressure on her burnt sternum. In the satchel Thade always wore around her waist, safely hidden under her robe, she'd even tucked away some moss soaked in a healing potion of mud, burning embers, and her own blood. Pesdari recalled the blissfully cool touch of the wet moss on her palms as Thade had tenderly tied it in place with leather straps.

The physical pain was always atrocious, but it was the dreams that came in the nights and days after that, Pesdari knew with unbridled certainty, that left a deeper mark upon the Ritual's participants. It was easy to estimate an end to the suffering of the body. With the proper balms, cleanings, and spells, the burns and blisters could clear up in about five days, but the dreams – the messages from the gods – those could go on for merely a day or as long as a month, depending on the caliber of sacrifice offered. But then again, the gods could be fickle. A person could never guess at their timeline. She had seen members of her coven spontaneously erupt into balls of flames that burned for hours or sunk into a puddle of mud for mere seconds, only to appear again completely unscathed — physically, at least. During these interludes, the gods spoke directly to those who had offered them a sacrifice, and while these blessed individuals would certainly emerge with a stronger magical prowess, you could always see something in their eyes, a nervous twitch or the stillness of a stagnant pool of water. There was a toll to these direct conferences with the gods.

Pesdari shook off an involuntary shudder as she thought of them, but it was not as if the gods distanced themselves from those who worshiped them through the practice of their magic. Sometimes the gods would descend in dreams to those they had, for some reason or other, taken a particular interest in. The whisperings of Tewar and Egal's shrieking voices could drive a person mad if they weren't prepared, but Pesdari was well-trained in the elements of water and wind. And while she was not the most talented in the study of the earth, she enjoyed the practice. Hetra's rumblings did not make her bones ache until she feared they'd break (as they did for some) as she slept but were almost soothing to her. It was Riefon's visitations that usually made her heart go black with fear and pain. She did not attend her lessons in fire with more energy than she needed to in order to complete a task. This impudence meant that the old god sometimes delivered punishment in the form of hideous nightmares where she was chased by flaming horses as a brittle voice crackled behind her. She was no stranger to the gods, but she could not even imagine how much more awesome it would be to stand directly before them.

Pesdari's reverie was broken by a harsh intake of breath from Thade.

"Pest…"

Pesdari tried to ask Thade what was wrong, but when she opened her mouth water spurted out of her lips all over Thade's face.

"Sit down, Pest!" Thade ordered, with an exasperated look in her eyes. "You're going to drop me."

Pesdari could barely hear or see Thade as she lowered her to the ground before laying down beside her. Salty water was welling in her eyes and sloshing in her ears. Involuntary panic was making her hyperventilate, but just then a profound warmth and tenderness flooded her being. She looked around and saw that she was no longer with Thade. She wasn't even within the Hall anymore. She had been transported to a place far beyond the confines of the coven. Surrounded by the bitter yet warm water on all sides, fish of dazzling colors flashed by her, and gorgeous creatures that Pesdari could not name stretched out their long tendrils to tickle her feet. The only sound she could make out was the low, undulating song of old

Tewar, rising from the deep dark water below her. She listened, almost hypnotized as the god gifted her with new secrets of the water. A current twirled her playfully as she listened to his enchanting song. She learned how to tell if water was clean enough to drink and how to encourage fish to flip out of rivers with just her fingertips.

A school of orange and daisy colored fish surrounded her. Fascinated, Pesdari lifted her hand to gently touch them as they swam by. A final, soft bellow from below caused her to look away from the fish. Something big was moving in the deep expanse. Curious, she flipped in the water and began to swim toward the shadowy figure. In the darkness, massive bright yellow eyes stared up at her. Pesdari was transfixed.

"Bewaaaaaare, deaaaaar ooooonne."

Pesdari wanted to ask what she was supposed to beware, but she never got the chance. The water gripped her, and she was madly hurled toward the surface. Her eyes and mouth opened wide in shock as a horrific pressure bore down on her skull and lungs. She feared she was about to die, that the gods didn't realize how fragile her human body was and would kill her as the water rushed by. But then she shot through the surface and kept sailing upwards toward a brilliantly sapphire sky. The pressure that had crushed her just before thankfully dissipated. A strong gust of wind swept her away and the next thing she knew, she was flying with the birds in the realm of Egal. Below her, a forest's treetops swayed. Joy exploded in her heart as she flitted about with little songbirds. Their shining eyes twinkled in the sunlight. She rolled onto her back, drifting like a feather. A falcon entered her line of sight for just a moment before tucking in its wings and plummeting down for a kill. With every rush of air, Pesdari began to catch snippets of words, soft plaudits, and whispered secrets of the wind. Egal whispered to her how she could harness the wind to remove obstacles in her path before her joy was interrupted by a gale force wind.

"All creatures must rest in death," Egal bit into her ear. "Remember this."

All of a sudden, Pesdari was lifted above the small feathered creatures and then even above the clouds. Strong winds thrust her higher and higher until she could no longer breathe, and the sky's tranquil blue was replaced by an all consuming darkness. A wide expanse of nothing, only silence, confronted Pesdari. The darkness before her was of a kind she had never seen. An oblivion that held none of the comforting familiarity of her gods or her coven, as terrible as they could be. Fear stormed throughout her being, but she was unable to move or even blink despite every instinct within her spiking with horror and desperation to escape this horrible dimension. And then Pesdari felt herself hurtling down, down, down. Her jaw was locked and her face was pulled back tight, but despite this, she was still grateful to be escaping that horrible void. Hideous snapping laughter echoed throughout her mind as she began to fall faster. Her face and hair erupted into flames.

"Were you frightened of the loneliness, little ember?" Seethed a voice in her ear. "Fear not, for I burn here too."

Then her whole body was suddenly consumed by fire, and she was transformed into the realm of Riefon. The acrid smell of burning hair incensed her nostrils. Her skin bubbled and flew away in patches. The pain was unlike anything she had ever felt before. She would have screamed if she'd been able, but the speed at which she descended made it impossible for her to even move her jaw. She felt as if she had burned for eternity as Riefon admonished her laziness towards his worship, but just before she crashed down into the realm of Hetra, he begrudgingly shared how to put fire in a bottle.

Suddenly, she was being embraced by sweet, damp earth. Mud cooled her aching flesh and long grasses caressed her affectionately. Pesdari realized she could move again so she stood. She saw she was in a meadow and felt a bubbling urge to play. She frolicked in the grass and laughed. She laughed so hard her stomach ached. A tremor shook through the ground, and Pesdari fell. She felt her body being sent rolling down a little hill, and when she stopped her travels, she found herself in soft dirt. As she rose to her feet, she felt more tremors erupt in her very bones, but there was no pain. Pesdari felt as if she were being tickled from the inside out. She could hear a voice calling too. It was a strong, booming voice, but she wasn't able to make out the words. She looked behind her and saw a cluster of treetops that for some reason she was certain was the Hall. Upon her realization that she was free, that she was in an unexplored field, and that she could run for miles in any direction with no barrier in sight, she broke out into ecstatic laughter once again. The unknown voice cut off her celebrations. She looked for the owner of the voice, and saw him several yards away.

A man with dark mottled skin was calling out to her and waving his arm as if inviting her over. Pesdari tried to take a step forward but found she could not move. The man once again waved his arm. She ordered her legs to run. Again, they refused to propel her forward, but instead emitted a wet, squelching noise. Pesdari looked down to find that her feet and ankles had been turned to mud. As she tried to yank what was left of her legs out of the mud, she realized she was no longer in the field but back in the Hall. A firm yet soft voice echoed in her head as she screamed.

"Mankind is of the mud and to the mud, mankind will return. Seal them in before their time with your own flesh and will."

She screamed again and heard a sharp voice in her ear.

"Shut up, Pest! You're here! You're back."

Pesdari snapped her head toward the sound and saw Thade laying next to her on the ground.

"You're back," Thade told her again, softer now. Pesdari's eyes rolled in her head like a maddened horse as she took in the all too familiar roof of the Hall and the barrier of tree trunks around her. She was, as Thade had said, back in the coven's stronghold. Before she could help herself, she let out a mournful wail as tears fell from her eyes.

Chapter 5

The Coven

Pesdari hurriedly sat up and wiped her eyes with the sleeve of her robe. Her hands were shaking. She took long, slow breaths to calm herself.

"Your blessing from Vedra came *very* late," Thade casually noted from her spot on the ground. Still not looking at her, Pesdari shrugged and focused on her breathing.

"He never liked me much. Maybe that had something to do with it," she finally replied, though there was a quaver in her voice. Thade snorted.

"As if the gods care enough about us to toy with things like that."

"How long have I been gone?" Pesdari asked. Thade pulled her lips down and her shoulders up.

"It felt like a long time, but that may have been because I'm cold, hurt, and aching for some food. You vomited water all over me. It was even coming out of your nose in the beginning. My robe is soaked, and I'm freezing!"

With a slight tremor in her hand, Pesdari took off her own robe. Unlike Thade, she wore a long tunic underneath it. The weather was getting cooler but providers of a sacrifice had to forgo their undertunic for fear it would burst into flames during the Ritual.

She helped Thade sit up and put the dry robe on her. Then

she puffed out five sharp breaths followed by one long exhale. A powerful rush of wind rattled the Hall's branches before it swirled around Thade, lifting her about a foot into the air. She grinned in delight, and Pesdari put out her arm to guide Thade to the ground. As her feet touched the floor, Thade laughed, "I remember when you could only summon up a sneeze's worth of wind."

"I still learned it faster than you," Pesdari replied with a wry grin.

Thade once more rested against Pesdari's shoulder, and the two young women began their shuffling journey out of the Hall yet again. Due to Thade's wounds and Pesdari's now unsettled mind, the pair were making slow work of their exit. They hadn't even reached the entryway to the Yard yet. They were half way there though, and Pesdari could see a few of their coven wandering past it, enjoying their time outside in the crisp air. The seasons were beginning to turn, and the air entered their lungs with a delighted snap as the leaves fell to form a beautiful carpet of crimson and marigold.

The Yard was as wide as the Hall was tall, but it too was surrounded by a tight wall of trees, so tight that even the littlest member of the coven couldn't slip through. Unlike the Hall though, there was no roof here. The sky was open to them. On sunny days, Yerfi and Koa, the coven leaders charged with sharing knowledge of the outside world, often taught their lessons here. At one far end sat the scraping beam and wringing pole where the coven would transform the hides of cave aselonies into leather.

Yerfi and Koa would take the finest pelts and travel out into the world beyond the trees. There they would trade the pelts in exchange not only for goods but for news of the wider world. These stories of the places beyond the trees were shared with all the coven upon their return.

"Be wary, little ones," Koa would say. "There is war and malice outside our home, and there are generals and mages who are desperate for our knowledge." Sometimes Koa and Yerfi would also bring home small circular stones engraved with odd little shapes and faces. Yerfi and Koa had explained that these stones were called coins and outsiders would use them for trade when they had no goods to barter with.

"You must know these things if you ever leave here," Yerfi would tell the younger children as their eyes filled with wonder. When she had been small, Pesdari used to beg Koa to take her with him on his travels.

"When you are ready, the doors of this coven will open for you. Until then, you will remain here," Koa would always tell her younger self. It was an answer that had infuriated Pesdari then and still did, but through her lessons in the coven she had learned that this place was a harbor for the old magic. Koa had told her that in the world outside the trees hardly anyone could practice the old magic as well as they did. That was why the coven existed to preserve these ancient arts. For how long the coven had been here, Koa could not tell her, but Arni, the leader in charge of sharing the stories of the coven, lectured that old magic had been protected here for at least a thousand years. All the coven kept the old magic alive and honored it by working with it and obeying its terms.

"What you will learn to do here could decimate a kingdom," Arni used to say severely to his little charges. "Our protective magic keeps anyone untrained in our ways, anyone who does not respect the awesome responsibility that comes with these powers, out. And it keeps us safe."

As Pesdari heaved breath into her body, Arni's words came back to her.

"*Keep us trapped is more like it,*" she thought bitterly.

Finally, the two young women were out of the Hall and crossing the Yard. A few of their coven stood nearby and watched the pair make their way to the entrance of the Burrows, the underground quarters of all who lived here.

"Getting a bit greedy, aren't you, Thade?" Called out a tall, lithe young woman. The gentle beauty of her hair floating around her face like a black cloud was a sharp contrast to her stern expression. Ignoring her, Pesdari and Thade pushed on, but Pesdari couldn't help thinking that the comment was true. Most years there were only one or two sacrifices and those, Vebra's assassination attempt being the exception, were usually the results of mutual hatred, kindled by a tightly enclosed space, getting out of hand. Thade's sacrifices though, had all been victims of calculated strikes and none of them had ever even so much as quarreled with Thade as far as Pesdari could remember.

Pesdari couldn't even fathom why Thade would be doing all this in the first place. The coven, through eons of communing with nature, had developed such a relationship with the gods that the powers of magic would be shared with the coven leaders through whispers and dreams. True, the knowledge obtained that way was never as potent or as powerful as what could be gained through a sacrifice but no blood was ever shed and the leaders would pass the secrets on to generation after generation. Pesdari glanced at Thade from the corner of her eye. What was she doing all this for?

"You may be getting strong, but you can't kill all of us!" Icetu spat out then.

"Well, I wouldn't waste my time with you, Icetu!" Thade retorted over her shoulder.

"Someone will get you in the end!"

Not really paying attention, Pesdari tried to continue on her way, but she realized that Thade had gone completely still. She tensed, unsure of what to do. Thade was staring at Icetu. Her black eyes were as empty as the darkness Pesdari had just stared into, but a detached, almost frightening smile had ripped across her face.

"For me there will be no end," Thade replied, but it wasn't her voice that Pesdari heard. It was a gust of piercing cold wind that nearly froze Pesdari and the others to the bone. Icetu's eyes widened either with fear or rage, Pesdari couldn't tell. She did, however, see Icetu painfully bend to the ground and dig her fingers into the earth. A tremor began to vibrate through the Yard.

The ground where Thade and Pesdari stood shook as if it meant to come undone beneath them. Thade glanced down at the violent earth before throwing back her head to laugh; it was a bitter and manic sound. Then her head snapped to attention, her long hair whipping in the wind, and she hissed. Pesdari saw small globs of spit fly from Thade's mouth.

As the globs flew through the air towards Icetu, they began to harden into ice and grew longer and more pointed as they traveled. Icetu released her hands from the dirt and fell back just in time. Three massive icicles stabbed into the ground, just where her hands had been. The ground stopped shaking. The icy wind went quiet.

"We're going!" Pesdari called out, shaking off the cold. "Stop being an idiot, Thade," she whispered grimly.

She dug her shoulder tighter into Thade's armpit, and with a blink, Thade's eyes returned to their usual liveliness. Her nose crinkled.

"As if Icetu could have done anything to me," she said loudly enough for everyone to hear. Pesdari shouldered her again.

"Come on," Pesdari muttered, watching Icetu stand up from the dirt. As she and Thade stumbled away, Icetu glared at them, rubbing at her fingers.

At last, they made it to the entryway of the Burrows. The mouth of the tunnel was about six feet high and dug out of a mound of dirt that rose before them. Pesdari and Thade walked down a smooth ramp that became the main tunnel lined with torches. Several smaller tunnels branched off of it. On their left was a narrow tunnel that led to the large sleeping quarters of the children who were either born to the coven or adopted into it.

As they walked past, Pesdari could hear some of the younger ones convincing their friends that if they all combined their strength, they *could* convince the earth in Udre's bed to turn to dust while he was sleeping. Thade must have heard the plot too, because she chuckled as they made their way further down the main tunnel.

Throughout the years, the Burrows had grown. With earth all around them, the coven did not need to reach out too far for the magic needed to dig out new rooms for those who wanted a bit more privacy. Two adult members working together could easily carve out a room that could house six people in as little as a few hours, complete with earth carved beds.

Some rooms even had tables rising out of the floor where stone pots would sit so a coven member could create new potions and tinctures. But bedchambers weren't the only thing down in the Burrows. There were rumors that secret tunnels and rooms existed where coven members who were smitten with each other could go and have a few private moments to themselves. Pesdari had never seen those tunnels or secret rooms but she didn't doubt they existed. She had no use for them though as none of those tunnels were said to lead out of the magical wall of trees. There was only one way out of the coven, and that was the only secret passageway she had any interest in.

When they finally arrived at Thade's dwelling, which was deep underground and well away from many of the other quarters, Pesdari let go of her and stood back. Like the other bedchambers, there was a humble wooden door fitted into a simple frame. Thade's door differed from the other doors though, because it was sealed in a thick, massive sheet of ice. The air in this section of the corridor was colder too, and Pesdari noticed that goosebumps had erupted along her arms.

Thade hobbled up to her icy door with her index finger extended. She took a deep breath before closing her eyes. Her finger began to glow red. When it was the color of a ripe apple, she ran her finger tip from the very top to the bottom of the door. Pesdari raised her eyebrows. Despite having gone through the Ritual and the skirmish just moments ago, Thade was still able to perform exhaustive feats of magic without any help from the elements — and without becoming too winded from it. Icetu was strong, but Thade was clearly stronger. Perhaps Thade had been correct in the Yard. Maybe Icetu really couldn't have done anything to her even in a weakened state like this.

There was a rush of water then as the ice that had once been four inches thick, cascaded down and flowed around their feet. Thade stepped back with a mournful look at her now soaked toes, her finger back to its usual color. She pushed the door. Looking her shoulder, she said, "There's no traps. It's safe. Sorry about the water," before walking inside. Pesdari followed her into the spacious chamber that, for the coven, was exquisitely furnished. A circular table rose from the floor in the center of the room. Wooden pegs emerged from the walls and beautiful dyed satchels hung from them. There was a pleasing smell of mint and thyme that wafted about the room.

Thade then groaned softly as Pesdari helped her onto her earthen bed carved into the wall in such a way that it had an earthen roof. A tapestry was tied to one side of the bed's opening, but if Thade wanted to, she could release the tapestry and hide herself away. Her bed was lined with aseloni skins. It also had pillows stuffed with goose feathers, treasures that the coven leaders Yerfi and Koa had brought back from their travels. A frown flicked at the edges of Pesdari's mouth. It wasn't that all the lovely things Yerfi and Koa brought back only went to the leaders of the coven, but these pillows were particularly fine and should have gone to one of the more senior members of the coven. Surely Divorc or even Rouble would have been given first choice at these. Thade must have done some favor for one of the coven leaders to have secured such niceties. Pesdari flinched as a voice hissed in the back of her mind.

"Beware of her," it cackled, sounding much like Riefon. Pesdari pushed the thought away as she watched Thade pull a woven blanket up to her chin.

"Thade, don't be stupid. I have to treat your wounds. Where's the healing poultice you made?" Pesdari asked, looking around the room. She didn't see the covered wooden bowl that held the necessary implement.

"I'm fine," Thade yawned. Pesdari frowned and reached out to pull the blanket away.

"Stop it!" Snapped Thade. She tried to slap Pesdari's hand away, but it was no use. Pesdari had the blanket in her grip and yanked. She stared in shock.

"You're... you're healing!" She sputtered. The savage burn that had scorched Thade's sternum barely an hour ago was already knitting itself back together. Despite it being such a recent addition to Thade's body, the burn now looked as if it had been treated and was already a day old. Thade wet her lips, casually looking away.

"Yes."

"I don't – how have you – how?" Pesdari stammered. Thade didn't answer. Pesdari shook her head, trying to clear it of her confusion. Such healing powers were nearly unheard of. There had been one such master of the healing arts in the coven, Atsmr, but he had been very old and did not have half of Thade's power in any other regard. The current coven leader who taught the healing arts, Koa, couldn't hold a candle to Thade's skill apparently. Thade was becoming quite formidable indeed. Pesdari snapped herself back into a cool expression. She moved and began to fiddle with a small clay bottle that sat on Thade's table.

"Well, I now understand how you recovered so quickly from the last Ritual," she said dryly, placing her thumb in position to pop the cork out of its place.

"I wouldn't do that," Thade warned lightly. With a look of

mild concern, Pesdari delicately put the bottle back down.

"What's in it?" she asked, whipping her hands against her tunic.

"I don't remember," Thade sighed. She waved her hand. "Probably something nasty. Everyone here's been irritating me lately so I've whipped up a few little things."

Pesdari used the tip of a finger to push the bottle further away from her. The two fell silent, but only for a moment.

"Why did you have to kill Delbon so quickly after the last one?" Pesdari asked.

Thade closed her eyes with an annoyingly tranquil smile and shrugged. Pesdari scowled.

"Don't do that. Tell me. You have something planned. I can tell. Are you working up the strength to leave?"

Pesdari had tried to remain impassive, but when she asked the question she couldn't restrain the agitation in her voice. Thade opened her eyes and shifted her gaze toward her friend. Her face was quizzical as she watched Pesdari.

"You really hate it here, don't you," she said, less a question and more a statement of fact.

"Getting out of here is the only goal I have," Pesdari answered, sitting on a rough hewn chair that sat opposite the bed. "Don't you want to get out at some point?"

Thade stared at the ceiling before replying, "I've spent all my twentyone summers here. I don't have memories of anywhere else like you do. I'm alive. I don't really care where I am as long as I can keep breathing."

"Well, I was seven summers old when I came here, and I've spent every one of my thirteen summers here wanting to leav —"

"—You know, Pesdari," Thade interrupted, "I don't remember the last time I saw you smile." Pesdari looked at her, flustered by the dramatic change in the subject.

"I-It-There isn't much to smile at in this place," she stammered. Thade scoffed, "That's just because you get more dour every winter. You're *alive* — that's worth a smile, isn't it?"

Pesdari scowled at her.

"We're *trapped* here, Thade, and those who aren't skilled enough to escape become sacrifices!"

Thade dismissed the argument with a wave of her hand.

"Is it so bad to sacrifice the weak? It's the only way they can become useful! Look at me! I'm already healed. It's only because of our ways that I've gained so much…," Thade trailed off as her slender fingers caressed her healing skin.

"Power," Pesdari finished for her. Thade rolled her eyes.

"I was going to say wisdom, but in any case, this is our home!"

"This may be your home but it's not mine," Pesdari retorted.

"As I am always telling you, Pest, this is *our* home, and you are my family," Thade responded. Her tone made it clear that she was tired of having to tell this to her friend again. Pesdari shook her head. Thade had been born into the coven, but Pesdari had once lived outside, free from the threat of sacrifice, in a place where the horizon stretched out before her and beckoned her to explore everything it held.

Once, long ago, she had never known she would be a student of the old gods. She was simply a little girl growing up with her mother in a small fishing village along the River Bounty. She could still vividly recall the day the Vuglar swept through her home like a storm. With their war cries and battle horns, they brought death and destruction.

Pesdari remembered the rubble that the Vuglar raiding party had left in their wake; rubble she and her mother had then laid in for hours. Her mother had been on top of her, almost crushing her, and Pesdari had felt something warm and wet seeping into her clothes. In a panic, she feared that she had wet herself and that the spreading mess would get on her mother too.

She whimpered, but when her mother gave no response, she forced herself to whisper, "Momma? Momma?"

Her mother still did not answer. Pesdari thought that it was shockingly quiet now that the clanging of swords and the echoes of screams had dispersed. Aside from the cries of carrion above, the only sound was her mother's haggard breathing. Then Pesdari's ears pricked up. She thought she could hear footsteps. Terror had filled her.

Were the Vuglar back? Was this something even worse? She had tried to hold her tears in check, but she hadn't been able to help herself. Pesdari had begun to sob. The steps became louder and Pesdari realized that whoever was here was coming towards her and her mother. She had screamed when she saw fingers grip her mother's shoulder.

"Leave her alone! Leave her alone!"

As her mother's weight was pulled off of her, Pesdari had jumped to her feet. She was ready to fight despite being just a little girl. In a panic, she whipped her head back and forth to find something, anything, that could be used as a weapon. On the ground was a long hunting knife, covered in blood. She had snatched it up and bared her teeth. What she had seen next left her stunned. There was a large man with a short black beard kneeling next to her mother as she gasped for air. Pesdari saw that a long gash ran along her mother's stomach and that her tunic had been nearly stained black with blood.

Her mother's eyes had been wild as she tried to raise a hand to strike the man, but he had simply taken her hand and held it gently. He had then looked from the woman before him to Pesdari and then surveyed the still burning huts and the bodies that littered the ground. Some were moaning but many were still and silent.

"Where is your family?" The man had asked Pesdari. She pointed to her mother.

"There is no one else?" He asked. Dazed, Pesdari slowly shook her head. The man sighed before turning back to her mother, whose hand he still held in his.

"Your child is safe. I come from the coven of Yrecep Forest. I will take her with me," he had told her mother. The woman's eyes no longer mirrored a trapped animal, now it seemed that she was having trouble even keeping them open.

"Your child is safe," the man repeated softly. "Go to your rest."

He then placed his other hand on the woman's chest. She had turned her head to look at Pesdari and tried to smile at her daughter. The man then pushed hard against her chest. Her back had arched and a sharp rush of air left her. As it did so, so too did the light in her eyes. Before the man spoke again, Pesdari had known her mother was gone. The man lowered the woman's lifeless hand to the ground. Pesdari kept her eyes transfixed on her dead mother as the man approached her.

"I am Koa. You will be one of us now."

The memory of how she had come to live in Yrecep Forest swirled in her mind. She could barely remember the River Bounty or her mother's voice, but she could never forget watching her die. Thade was speaking, "Everything in life is fascinating to me. Death is the greatest waste."

Pesdari blinked, confused.

"Wha-what were you saying?"

Thade shot her an annoyed look, but softened when she saw the distracted air in Pesdari's eyes.

"I'm glad Koa brought you here," Thade murmured. Pesdari looked at her. Thade had been the only one Pesdari would tolerate in those early days. And this was mainly due to Thade's insistence that the two of them would be friends. When Pesdari would cry in the night, wailing for her mother, little Thade would cuddle her. She would tell her stories about her own dead mother who had succumbed to an illness the summer before.

"It is alright that our mommas are gone. We will take care of each other," Little Thade would say. As the years rolled by, the two seemingly did everything together. When they were twelve summers old, Thade would braid Pesdari's hair and sigh about how she couldn't wait for one young boy or another to notice her. Pesdari would snort and call her an idiot. And while Pesdari at first had been afraid of the magic wielded by the coven, she soon became quite a skilled practitioner herself. She and Thade would while away the hours, practicing their magical skills or pretending they were the old gods come to wrack destruction on all those unfortunates who had made them mad that week. Sometimes the game would go a little too far and the pair would actually enact their revenge for pretty grievances. Needless to say, the other children learned to keep their distance.

Thade held Pesdari dear to her heart, but Pesdari couldn't shake her intense longing for freedom, a prize for which she would pay any price. She would be free of this place someday.

"I-Thade—"

Thade cut the sentence short with a wave of her hand.

"I'm going to sleep. Go catch some fish in the caves or something. If you bring me dinner tonight, I'll trade you some mead for it."

Pesdari nodded and rose. The caves were the only way out of the coven. When she'd only been thirteen summers old, she had spied on Koa when he and Yerfi gathered pelts and fish to trade with the outsiders. They had gone into the Hall, walked past the Ritual leader's mound and down the stone steps behind it. Pesdari used a trick she had learned to be silent as she followed them into the Hall. With every step she asked the ground to muffle her step, and so she had tailed the coven leaders like a shadow down the steps that led to the underground caves.

The caves were vast and a river rushed through the subterranean system. The only light came from torches that lined the stone walls. The coven would regularly congregate at this river to fish for the translucent, large fichtacs that swam in its currents. They were not simple prey. The long barbels that trailed from their faces were dangerous. A sting from one would immobilize the small dryprinics that they loved to eat. If an unfortunate human were to be stung, the poison could fester and cause a rot in the affected site unless it was properly treated, but the fictacs weren't the only predators in the river.

The cave aselonis, with their sharp teeth and huge bulbous eyes, also used the river as their feeding ground. While lounging and socializing on the rocks, they looked a bit ridiculous. Their enormous bulk would bounce back and forth as they slapped their strong flippers against the ground to push themselves forward. In the river, however, they could propel themselves at breakneck speeds, their powerful jaws snapping up even the mightiest fichtacs.

Cunning as they were fast, the cave aselonis would often work together to herd the fish toward disaster. Dark as night, they could conceal themselves in the caves and snap at unsuspecting passersby. In the dim light of the torches, they could barely be seen, but their teeth and eyes would sparkle in the dark like menacing stars. It was rare, but children wandering off on their own in the dark would sometimes stumble upon ill-tempered aseloni, and if they could not escape in time, they suffered the consequences.

Young Pesdari had tried to keep up with the coven leaders as they made their way through one cavern after another, but the tunnels that connected the caverns twisted and turned in the dark. No sooner had she lost them did she realize that she too was lost. It had taken her two days to find her way back to the Hall, hungry and miserable and a bit terrified. While she had the good luck to never run into it, she had heard something rumbling not so far away from her. The echoes of its movements would send her into trembles, and she would be sent running, only to trip and fall into small pools of water that had collected from the drippings of the stalactites that lined the ceilings of the cave.

Pesdari still explored the caves from time to time, now that she could coax the flame of a torch to burn longer than it normally would, but she was always careful to mark her path so she could find her way back. This trip to the caves though would require no special effort. She did not plan on any excursions today. She stood in the doorway, the daylight illuminating just the tips of some of the cavern's sharp stony teeth, and then down the stone steps she walked, down into the glittering dark.

Chapter 6
The Bargain

Pesdari stood on the stony riverbank, a net clasped in her hand. The sound of the rushing water filled her ears, but her empty stare did not drink in the sight of the river before her, even though the purple crystals that lined its bed made the surface twinkle majestically under the torchlight. Pesdari was sunk deep into the recesses of her mind.

She thought of the warnings the gods had given her. In the maelstrom of her vision, she hadn't really paid any heed to them, but now that her spirit was a bit more settled she couldn't help but mull over their meaning. It was strange that they had said such things to her. Something dangerous was surely afoot, she thought, but why had the gods delivered such a message to her out of everyone in the coven?

As far as she had known from her own experience and the shared tales of others, the gods simply imparted some slight bits of magical knowledge and never shared more than what was fitting. Of course, there were stories of past coven members who had been particularly skilled at communing with the gods and could even reach out to the mystical beings in dreams for guidance without undergoing the Ritual, but Pesdari did not flatter herself.

She knew she did not possess the skills or even the inclination to willingly seek out more audiences with the gods than she had to. Her lips flattened into a tight line. Their warnings were troubling, but even more disturbing was that they apparently had something to do with her. Being the focus of the gods' attention, she thought, was deeply unsettling.

Before she could contemplate the matter further, a haggard voice sounded from the dark.

"Kill her for me."

Pesdari snorted as she cast out her net into the river. She had just arrived at the riverbank and already she was being bothered.

"That is a bold request," she replied dryly, not bothering to look behind her. She already had a fair idea of who was lurking in the inky shadows. As she suspected, Evlor emerged from a dark crevice and stepped into the light of a nearby torch. The flames danced across her cedar colored face, but her eyes remained dark with malice.

"Is it?" she asked. Pesdari frowned over her shoulder at Evlor before turning her eyes back towards the outstretched net. She returned Evlor's question with one of her own.

"Why should I help you?"

Evlor moved closer until she stood beside Pesdari. She gazed out over the rushing water. The pair were quiet for a moment as the river flowed by, unaware of their existence. Then Evlor spoke.

"A sacrifice the caliber of Thade would bring you such a blessing from the gods. Think of the secrets you could learn. She's already performed the Ritual four times in as many weeks." Evlor's voice as she continued dripped with hatred. "She's like a pregnant aseloni. Filled to the brim and too bloated to run."

As if they heard themselves mentioned, the cave aselonis began to bray. Farther up river, there was a splash as one of them dropped into the water.

"And like a pregnant aseloni, she is much more dangerous when cornered," Pesdari frowned. "I also don't feel any ill will towards her as you do. Kill her yourself."

"I can pay you," Evlor countered. Pesdari scoffed at the offer.

"Why should I risk my life for your revenge? Leave me alone. I'm trying to catch my dinner." Pesdari folded her arms across her chest, shivering slightly. She scowled. She had been so unsettled by today's events that she had forgotten her robe in Thade's chambers. The air was quite cool in the caverns, and a chill was running along her unclad arms.

"What I can give you is worth the risk," Evlor pressed on, refusing to back down.

"And what is that?" Pesdari drawled, trying with every fiber in her being to demonstrate how clearly uninterested she was in this whole affair.

Evlor ignored her question and instead, much to Pesdari's irritation, gave instructions on how she would like Thade's assassination to be conducted.

"Drown her slowly. Let her gasp for air and think she has a chance to survive."

"How can you pay me? Why are you even asking this of me?" Pesdari asked again, now with an edge to her voice. She did not like having her time wasted. Evlor should just spit out her worthless offer so she could reject it and be done with this utterly idiotic conversation. In no world would she go up against Thade, especially not after what she had just learned about Thade's magical prowess.

Evlor tilted her head in Pesdari's direction but did not meet her gaze.

"You're the only one Thade trusts," she murmured. Then her hands curled into fists at her side. Pesdari thought she could detect a slight quiver in Evlor's voice when she spoke again.

"Delbon found the way out of the caves."

Pesdari's face flushed cold when she heard that. The way out — no, it couldn't be true.

"Do this for me, and I will tell it to you," Evlor said, her voice strong again.

Pesdari stared hard at Evlor, searching for any sign of treachery. A despairing woman was dangerous to make deals with when she no longer cared about her own life. She took in a deep breath through her nose and gently blew the air in Evlor's direction. She was far stronger when working with water, but Pesdari had studied quite hard at this particular trick of air, and she was grateful she finally had an opportunity to use it. Evlor's long, tightly woven strands of hair danced in the soft rush of air that flitted about her. As Pesdari sucked the inquisitive wind back into her lungs, a swell of knowledge permeated throughout her. Truth. Evlor was telling the truth. Pesdari was silent, trying to keep herself calm.

"Tell me first," she said.

"No," Evlor replied, but, as if she were prepared for this haggling, she continued quickly before Pesdari could object. "But I will tell you where our supplies are hidden. They're yours."

Pesdari could barely keep from scowling; she knew it would have been too easy to simply be given the information she wanted, but she still was irritated that it wasn't immediately handed over upon request.

"And?"

"And after you kill Thade, I will tell you how to leave the coven," Evlor told her.

Pesdari's heart was threatening to break through her ribs, but she kept her voice even as she asked, "Why don't you leave if you know the way out?"

Evlor gestured to the glistening cave walls that surrounded them both.

"Delbon is a part of this place now. I can never leave her," she said softly. Then she turned and looked hard at Pesdari. "Thade thinks you are her friend, but I have seen you. You care for no one. You know nothing of love."

Pesdari's lip curled.

"Love is a risk in this place," she said, quoting Thade. "One that can get you sacrificed," she spat. Evlor drew close then, her eyes as fiery as the torches.

"Then do this for me and leave here! Escape before someone makes you their sacrifice. Before *Thade* comes for you. You're a strong magic user. She's clearly targeting those who are skilled. You could very well be next."

Pesdari set her mouth into a firm line as she considered the bargain. Delbon had been smart, quite clever really. If anyone could have found their own way out of the caves, it would have been her. This was a rare chance, and, in all likelihood, she did have to consider that Thade was harvesting as much as she could take. Perhaps Evlor was right. Perhaps no one was safe from Thade's ambitions. Pesdari stared back into Evlor's eyes.

"I'll do it," she said. "Now tell me where the supplies are."

Evlor nodded and pointed upriver.

"Delbon dropped enchanted stones to guide the way. You only need to whisper to them and they will glow. That will lead you to the supplies."

"Whisper what?" Pesdari pressed. She was not going to be conned during this exchange. Evlor shrugged.

"Anything you like. Best if you're polite though."

Pesdari nodded to herself. So Delbon had used Hetra's magic to enchant the stones. Famously, Hetra's magic didn't take to rough language well. The older coven members would try to warn frustrated younglings not to verbally abuse the old god too much as they attempted to dig out caverns or carve out earthen shelves on their own. If they didn't heed the warnings and cursed or berated their materials anyway, the dirt would more than likely end up bursting into dust, leaving the young magic users temporarily blinded and spitting out dirt. Younglings would quickly learn to respect their materials.

"And what did you pack?" Pesdari asked, desperately hoping that what the two young women squirreled away was worth this bloody bargain.

"Enough food and water for five days of travel. We used to study how much Yerfi and Koa would pack for themselves."

"I see," Pesdari breathed. Her mind was racing at the thought of finally being free from the coven. That would surely be adequate for one person traveling alone. For a fleeting moment she considered killing Evlor where she stood and running off into the dark. Then she saw the knife at Evlor's hip. While she could very easily have called upon the river water to drown Evlor, it wouldn't have happened instantly. Evlor would have plenty of time to slash at her, and Pesdari was no healer like Thade. They would most likely both die for nothing if Pesdari made a move to attack.

"When will you kill her?" Evlor curtly asked, interrupting her thoughts.

"Give me a few days. Now go. It's probably best that no one sees us together."

Evlor turned and began to walk towards the stairs that led to the Hall.

"Remember, Pesdari... make it slow," she said. Pesdari stared at her retreating form. Then, at long last, she turned back to her net. As she began to haul in it, she wondered how she would kill her one and only friend.

Chapter 7

The Secret Room

Thade wasn't in her quarters when Pesdari returned. She warily looked about the room before lowering her meager catch to the floor. After Evlor had left her alone by the river, she could think of nothing else but the possibility of freedom. Her spirits soared while her stomach simultaneously twisted into anxious knots.

The murder of a friend was certainly a high price to pay for her escape from the coven, and yet, the guilt she had felt was rather unimpressive compared to the worry that it was she who might end up dead instead. It was highly probable that she would get herself killed on this mad venture. Listening to the aselonies bray, she had entertained the thought of simply stealing the supplies and then trying to find her way out on her own, but the idea was quickly squashed. Even if she had enough food and water for five days without the faintest hint of which direction she should follow, there was a very high chance that she would get lost and perish in the caves. The twisting caverns held more than bad tempered aselonies, she was sure of it.

No stranger had ever entered the coven unless they had been accompanied by Koa and Yerfi, but it stood to reason that after all these years someone from the outside must have found the entrance to the caves, perhaps by mistake or in a desperate attempt to be reunited with a lost child. And yet, no one had ever made their way to the Hall or the Burrows. Pesdari surmised that something lurked in the dark that ended their travels and, most likely, their lives as well. Unable to concentrate on anything else, she had cut short her fishing expedition and returned to Thade's chamber.

Now, as she looked around the empty room, fear welled up within her, and her left eyelid began to twitch. Her heart raced. Where was Thade? Had she somehow spied on her conversation with Evlor? Did she already know of the plot? Pesdari thought she heard a noise and whipped around, ready to defend herself. There was nothing. The room was empty and quiet. She breathed in deep to calm her nerves. As powerful as Thade may be, she wasn't all-knowing. At least, she hadn't shown any signs of being so yet. Pesdari resolved that it would be best to prepare dinner as requested and not to act rashly. Her time would come.

As she crouched down to cook the meal, one large fichtac, she noticed that next to a carved earthen shelf, a full aseloni bladder was hanging from a peg that stuck out from the wall. The shelf held two plain wooden dishes and a cup. She got up to inspect the bladder and was pleased to discover water inside and not another of Thade's strange concoctions. She could use this, she thought with a thin smile. Pesdari then felt a pit in her stomach as she imagined watching Thade die before her, drowning from magically contorted water. She grimaced, but then hardened her heart.

"*No*," she thought. "*No remorse.*"

This was her chance at escape, and she would take it, friendship be damned. She took a plate from the shelf and set it on Thade's table before returning to the fish. She began rubbing her palms together faster and faster until steam rose from her flesh. Gritting her teeth, she moved her now smoldering palms along the fichtac. The smell of cooking fish swelled through the room, and the sizzling of her dinner caused her stomach to rumble in anticipation. Pesdari was not an ardent student of fire; her body paid the consequences of her negligence. Her palms began to sizzle along with the fish, but she used the pain in her hands to burn any sense of shame from her mind. Thade would have done the same to her, she thought, if such an opportunity was on the line. Now that the fish was cooked through, Pesdari spat on her hands and pressed them to the dirt floor in order to cool them.

"*Help me*," she thought. Instantly, the ground under her palms transformed into mud. The cool sensations soothed her brutalized skin. Her lips pulled down at the corners and her brow furrowed. Where *was* Thade? It was strange for her to be gone so long, especially since she knew food would be on the way. Pesdari stepped out of Thade's room and looked out into the corridor, back the way she had come. Seeing nothing of interest, she took a few steps to the right. Thade's chamber was one of the last rooms in this tunnel, but it did lead a bit further and curved into darkness, ready for a new room would be carved out for whatever reason some day.

Pesdari moved forward cautiously and then froze just at the bend in the tunnel. She could hear a faint voice. Disoriented, she assumed she must be hearing an echo from the other direction because as far as she could see the tunnel led to a dead end. The sound came again. It did not seem so far away now, and Pesdari didn't think that she was hearing the drifting of words through the air. It was a moan.

Her brows knit together in both consternation and concern as she focused on the voice. She moved towards the wall of earth that stood before her. The voice was still muffled, but she could tell she was drawing closer to its source. Pesdari pressed her ear to the wall, and her mouth opened in surprise. The voice was clearer now. Once more a pitiful, sad moaning reached her ears. Was this one of the secret rooms Pesdari had heard about as a youngling? Curious, she quickly began to run her fingers along the wall, trying to suss out where the magically concealed opening could be.

All of a sudden her fingers trembled as they grazed one section of earth. She gasped. Her fingertips were practically vibrating with magic. Was Thade in there with someone? If Thade was distracted, then this could be the perfect moment to strike. Her ear pressed against the wall, greedy for knowledge of Thade's presence. Then she heard it, muffled certainly, but it was Thade's voice she was sure of it.

"Be still... Pest will be... soon."

A frisson of excitement ran through Pesdari's flesh. Thade was distracted by someone in there. Reluctantly, she pulled her hand from the wall; the magic emanating from it was so strong that it was practically intoxicating. She felt light headed as she stepped away but shook herself into focus. She ran back to Thade's room and, after hesitating for just a moment, snatched the aseloni bladder from its peg. She draped it over her head so the strap fell across her front, and the bladder was secured between her left arm and her side. She rushed back, hoping she still had time to execute her plan.

Upon her return, she pressed her front flat against the enchanted wall. The earth was cool against her cheek. She stretched her arms out wide. She looked as if she were trying to embrace the structure. While she wasn't sure what type of enchantment had been used, she was certain there was someone behind the wall and that must mean that there was a room, so she felt rather confident in how to sneak through. Pesdari began to whisper to the dirt, asking for entry into the secret room. She layered nicety upon nicety in hopes of a quick response. She waited for a moment, and then her heart leaped as she felt the earth begin to move around her face and her arms as it slowly swallowed her whole. She was being passed through numerous layers of dirt and rocks.

The crushing pressure bore down upon her until the air was forced from her lungs, and she would have cried from the agony if she could have, but she was one with the earth now; it gave her no space to even expand her lungs. Suddenly, she was unceremoniously squeezed out into a small room. Pesdari fell to her knees, gasping for air. She immediately felt for the aseloni bladder. Like her, it had emerged from the dirt unscathed. Grabbing at the wall, she pulled herself upright and surveyed the room. She had thought she was prepared for her task, but she was frozen in shocked silence by the sight that greeted her.

A boy, a mere youngling, was tied down to a black, rectangular stone table that came up a little higher than Pesdari's stomach. His face was turned away from her, focused on a narrow doorway that led to a second chamber. She heard a moan creep out of his mouth and realized that it was his voice that had first drawn her in, not Thade's or a lover's. Her mouth went dry. She narrowed her eyes as she peered at him. What strange happenings had she interrupted, and who had done this to the youngling?

The stone table was enough to catch Pesdari off guard. Creating tables and beds from the earth was relatively easy after a few practices, but magically carving creations from stone required a great deal more energy and time. There were a few small stone pots and basins scattered throughout the quarters for communal cleaning and potion making, but if a large cauldron was needed, such an item was usually carved directly into the cave walls where there was plenty of natural material available.

As she stared at the table, Pesdari was sure she would have noticed someone creating such a massive thing, or at the very least, she certainly would have seen it being transported all the way from the caves to the Burrows. No, whoever made this structure was incredibly powerful and had enough control to command every bit of rock and stone to arise from their places deep within the ground and assemble where they now stood.

Pesdari sniffed. There was a strong metallic scent in the air. She moved closer to the youngling, and her eyes went wide. A thin hollow reed stuck out from the inside of his elbow, and his blood dribbled out into a shallow wooden bowl that sat on the ground. It was nearly full. This was like no blood letting Pesdari had ever seen before. On occasion, when certain diseases struck, Koa would bring the fat and fanged eleches which would be used to greedily suck away infected blood. Nothing so refined as what Pesdari stared at was utilized by the coven.

She drew her eyes away and saw that sharp stone knives of varying sizes rested near the youngling's feet. As she quickly scanned the room, she was taken aback by the strange array of ingredients, potions, and large number of glass bottles that held dismembered body parts from both humans and beasts. The coven had acquired a glass bottle or two from the outside world, but such an object was precious and safely tucked away in the confines of the leaders' quarters. Pesdari's jaws pressed tight together. If this was all the doing of one of the coven leaders, she knew she would be in for a fight, one that she might not win. Despite this, she couldn't help but stare at the contents of the bottles.

The appendages were suspended in cloudy liquids. Pesdari shuddered in revulsion as she realized many of them still twitched and moved as if freshly severed. Whoever was doing this was tampering with magic that was... unnatural. In a dark corner of the room, she thought she saw yellow eyes staring at her. A voice whispered in her head.

"*Beeeeewwwaaaaaree.*"

Pesdari flinched as she recognized the deep echoes of that voice. Tewar was speaking to her, not in a vision or a dream but in her own reality. Something very wrong was going on here. She moved forward to touch the boy's shoulder. When he looked at her, Pesdari nearly screamed. Below his eyes sat the yellow muzzle of a dog. The fur continued onto his human cheekbones although with far less density. A large black nose twitched, but a taught leather strap kept his jaws shut. Pesdari's own mouth was open in abject horror. This *thing* that lay before her went against all that the coven taught and believed.

While they learned how to manipulate the natural world around them to their advantage by turning loose dirt into smoothed beds or water into ice — all these things could happen in nature on their own. The essence of their material was never fractured; however, warping natural materials, be it blood and bone or fire and ice, into a person's own perverse creations went against every rule the coven held dear. While they may murder each other for strength, the coven worshiped nature as it was, a hardened circle of life and death that held all the elements and creatures together in their own place. Death was not viewed as a crime but as a necessary part of life. Whatever this thing was though, Pesdari knew it went against nature, and whoever did it must be destroyed.

Swallowing her shock and fear, Pesdari turned her attention to the narrow doorway. She could hear chanting coming from the second chamber, and with an icy chill, she realized it was Thade. She edged closer to the entrance and saw Thade kneeling down before a child, another young boy with wild curly hair. She was just about to bind his hands when the boy slammed his head into her nose. Shouting in pain, Thade rose and stumbled through the narrow doorway. She was clutching her nose; blood flowed from her nostrils and dripped onto the floor. Pesdari froze. They gaped at each other. Still holding her nose, Thade opened her mouth to speak.

"How did you-"

She never finished her sentence. An unseen force sent her flying forward. As Pesdari scrambled out of her way, she caught a glimpse of the boy in the doorway, his head lowered to present thick curved horns.

"*Horns. He has horns!*" Pesdari thought, flabbergasted. The boy rushed to the table and began to tug at the other captive's binds.

"Thade, what have you done?" Pesdari managed to croak,

gripping the bladder close to her chest. Her mind was unable to comprehend the madness that was unfurling before her. Thade rolled onto her back, propping herself up on her elbows. Her face stained with blood.

"Stop them, Pesdari! My experiments!" she cried. She stared at Pesdari, desperate for help. For a moment, Pesdari saw the child's face that Thade once wore. Round cheeks and delicate eyes filled with trust for no one but her. Pesdari's mouth went dry. With trembling fingers, she removed the stopper from the bladder.

"I'm-I'm sorry," she murmured. The youngling slid off the table, and the little boy pulled him away from the two young women.

"What are you doing!" Thade shrieked. "Grab them!" She rose to her feet.

Pesdari closed her eyes and remembered how the water had enveloped and twirled her in her vision. She aimed the bladder at Thade and squeezed. The water rushed out violently and shot across the space toward Thade. When it reached her, it enclosed her head in a near perfect sphere. No matter how much Thade convulsed or whipped her body, she couldn't shake off the ball of water that was drowning her. Pesdari wasted no time; she ran to the enchanted earth wall. As she pressed her body once more against the dirt, she began desperately begging for release from the room. Thankfully, Hetra's magic took to her pleas, and the dirt once more began to swallow her. Just as her face was being submerged, she felt hands gripping to her back. She tried to free herself but it was too late. Whoever had grabbed her was coming too.

Once again, an immense pressure began to weigh down upon her, but this time the pain was amplified by panicked fingers that dug deep into her flesh. As the earth spat her out, she fell flat onto her stomach. Crushed by the weight on her back, she wriggled and bucked trying to free herself. Finally, she tossed off her hangers-on and crawled away. After clambering to her feet, she looked at what had come out of the room with her. She saw the young boy with a dog's muzzle and beside him knelt a younger boy whose thick curly hair barely hid a pair of goat's horns.

"Come on, Anicen," the little horned boy pleaded, tears running down his face. "Get up! Get up!"

Anicen whimpered but when he looked at the little boy, Pesdari saw his eyes take on a determined look. He gripped the little boy's hands and rose to his feet. A wave of dust clouded Pesdari's vision as the tunnel wall exploded. Squinting, she could make out a shape in the debris. It rushed forward and punched her in the jaw. She kept her feet, but she was discombobulated and couldn't resist as she was pulled towards the shape. The dust began to settle, and Pesdari saw Thade glowering at her with eyes swirling with rage.

"You," she hissed. Pesdari stared in horror as Thade tried to punch her again. She grabbed at Thade's wrist.

"What have you *done*?" she asked Thade again.

"I am obtaining immortality!" Thade screamed as she drew back her free hand, which was now wearing a flaming glove. Pesdari balked.

"What?" she gasped.

"We could have defied death!" Thade cried, furious tears streaking her cheeks. "We could have lived forever. But you! You *betrayed* me."

Thade raised her fiery hand, ready to slap it down on Pesdari's face. Pesdari let go of Thade's wrist and tried to move away, but Thade caught her tunic.

"Thade, no!" Pesdari shook her head. "No!"

She twisted and kicked, but Thade held her in an iron grip. She could not break free. She squeezed her eyes shut. There was a snarl and then a scream. Pesdari opened her eyes to see Anicen sinking his pointed fangs into Thade's arm. Quickly, she yanked herself free as Anicen released his bite and the little horned boy whipped around, getting between her and Thade.

Lowering his head, he charged at Thade, hitting her square in the stomach. The wind was knocked out of her, and she doubled over. Anicen was leaning against the wall, clearly exhausted. In Pesdari's head, the great voice of Hetra rumbled, *"RUN."*

Without thinking, Pesdari grabbed Anicen, and her feet began to churn beneath her.

"Come on!" she shouted over her shoulder at the other little boy who began to scramble after her. All three of them turned a corner just as an immense fireball exploded behind them; the tunnel they had just escaped from was rapidly transformed into a swirling inferno. The trio flew through the Burrows, running for their lives. Finally, Pesdari could see light from the entrance winking at them. She didn't have the time or the inclination to warn the rest of the coven about the murderous rage blazing through the tunnels toward them. As they rushed past one of the quarters, she heard someone call out, "What's going on?"

There was a flash of heat followed by a piercing scream. Pesdari kept running. Even if she had wanted to raise the alarm and warn the others, she wouldn't have been able to. Phrases and words meant nothing to her now. There was only a primal instinct driving her forward. Her body and mind were aligned with the one supreme goal of survival. At last they reached the entrance of the Burrows. The dog-faced boy Pesdari held in her grip yelped and began to stumble.

"Anicen!" shrieked their horned companion, but Pesdari hadn't lost her footing. Before the youngling hit the ground, she let out a piercing whistle. In an instant, a strong rush of hot wind slammed into their backs. A screech ripped through Pesdari's mind.

"Fly!"

They all were lifted an inch off the ground as the wind shot them out of the Burrows and into the Yard. Their feet were moving before they even touched the ground, and they rushed towards the Hall. The explosive sounds of Thade's rage had stopped. Pesdari glanced over her shoulder. Her former friend stood in the entrance of the Burrows, a fiery mask dancing over her face. The flames spread all over her body, until just an outline of her original form could be seen.

Thade shone light blue in the center of the fire, the flames that drew away from her burned with bold reds and yellows. From her head grew long, pointed horns of fire. Thick, gray smoke and horrible screams of those trapped inside the Burrows billowed out behind her. Some members of the coven were still out in the Yard. They all stood silent, frozen at the awesome sight. Thade pointed at Pesdari.

"I WILL BE ETERNAL!" Thade declared, her voice a funeral pyre's wretched roar. She spread her arms out wide. Fire spread from her fingertips and raced along the ground until it caught the roots of one of trees that lined the Yard. The fire snapped in delight, and the tree began to burn. Someone shouted and a spear of water flew at Thade. It sizzled into steam as soon as it got close to her. She laughed as she began to rise off of the ground, "LOOK ON ME! I WILL NEVER KNOW DEATH!"

She floated towards a coven member who meant to smother her fire with a wall of dirt. With a flick of her hand, she sent the debris flying, crushing two younglings as she did so.

"Thank you for your sacrifice," she cackled before she plucked the unfortunate being off the ground. Thade turned to look at Pesdari as she opened her mouth and bit into the burning flesh that had once been a throat.

Chapter 8

The Cave

Rouble burst from the Burrows, roaring. Her flesh, from head to toe, had been turned to stone. Her eyes glittered from her impervious face. She paused for a second, looking like an intricate statue, something only a true craftsman could have made. Breaking the illusion, she rushed at Thade and yanked the young woman's blazing figure to the ground.

Pesdari didn't stay to watch the fight. She fled to the Hall; the shouts and cries from the rest of the coven as they all began to do battle swelled in her ears like a storm. Pesdari didn't stop running once she reached the relative safety of the Hall, despite knowing that the two boys had slowed their pace to gather their breath. Her duty to them was finished. She had freed them from Thade's room of horrors. Their lives were in their own hands now. Glancing over her shoulder she thought, *"Good — they'll buy me time."*

She nearly flew through the structure and disappeared behind the speaker's mound. The boys paused in the doorway, panting. Anicen whined nervously before he scurried toward the speaker's mound. Staring back at him was a gaping black hole. Anicen snarled, then whipped his head around and barked. The little goat-horned boy moved quickly towards him. Anicen watched as his companion shifted nervously.

"Down there?"

CRACK.

A massive, burning tree limb now blocked the Hall's entrance and drowned out the little boy's shrieks. The two freed captives stared at the crackling limb, knowing that going back outside meant walking into a raging battle and fire. They turned to each other, both understanding they had no choice. With a nod, the pair began to run once more and followed Pesdari into the dark caverns.

When they caught up with her, they found Pesdari standing still by the river, whispering urgently to herself. The little boy, whose horns shimmered in the torch light, drew close, wondering what she was doing. As he glanced over his shoulder, he could hear the faint echo of screams drifting down the stone steps. Fear wreaked havoc in his stomach; he severely wanted to keep moving. Now that he was freed from that awful chamber of tortures, he wanted nothing more than to run far, far away where he could hide and forget all about this place. Nearby, Anicen had fallen to his knees and was furiously lapping at the water, but Pesdari didn't even register the boys' existence.

"Please, please, please, please show me the way out. Show me the way, and I will complete any task for you. Just please, please, please show me the way," Pesdari begged. Her eyes were closed tight, and her hands curled into fists. She continued her harsh whispering until she jumped at the little boy's yelp. He squeaked, "The rocks are glowing!"

Pesdari's eyes snapped open. The little boy with goat horns was right. Small pebbles shimmered like iridescent fish scales upon the ground. A trail of them led along the river bank. Relieved, she relaxed her jaw, but when she looked at the boys, she scowled.

"They followed me?" she thought. *"What do I do with them now?"*

After a moment, she huffed and snapped, "Come with me." Turning on her heel, she began to jog along the path of shimmering stones. With horror, the little horned boy noticed that every stone she passed blinked out into darkness. He frantically tugged at Anicen who drew his dripping jaws out of the river with only mild resistance. They rushed to keep up with Pesdari. The trio traveled briskly in silence for several minutes, carefully picking their way over rocks and guarding their steps from slippery stones. As the sounds of the fighting grew fainter, Pesdari whispered to the little boy, "You. What is your name?"

"Capar," he said quietly. "This is my brother Anicen. What's your name?"

"Pesdari. How did you come to be here?"

"That witch got us when we ran into Yrecep Forest to hide from the Vuglar."

Pesdari froze, shocked by his words.

"Thade found you in the woods?"

"Well, not her. Some older lady did. She said she would keep us safe. She gave us water, and... and then we fell asleep," Capar said. He shuddered as he continued, "When we woke up we were in that room."

Pesdari began to walk again. Her suspicions were confirmed. One of the coven leaders had been bringing back all manner of treasures and ingredients for Thade's experiments with immortality. How Thade planned on living forever, Pesdari still had no idea. She paused just before a ledge. She looked to her left. One last torch burned there. If she were to continue, they would have no light left to guide them. She looked down at her feet and cursed Thade for putting her in this situation. Then, she took off her slippers and picked them up. She held them close enough to the torch so just the toes caught alight. As she placed them carefully on the ground, she inhaled, her lungs ballooning under her bones. With cheeks as swollen as a frog's, she exhaled slowly as she walked in a circle around the slippers, which, to Capar's amazement, began to float into the air. Just as she was about to expel the last bit of air from her lungs, she blew it onto the fingers of her left hand. She waved her hand to the right, the burning slippers moved to the right. She moved her hand in a circle. The slippers followed the movement again.

She said, a bit smugly, "Alright, it's tethered to me now. We'll have light as long as the shoes burn. We should be able to see a little better."

The two boys stared, transfixed. Capar almost had a smile on his face. Pesdari glanced over their heads, back the way they had come and was thankful to see that no one was following them — yet.

"*At least Thade will still be trapped here even if she kills everyone*," Pesdari thought ruefully. She turned and began to walk before asking Capar, "Did you always... did *she* give you those horns?"

Capar did not respond. He touched his horns absentmindedly.

"She did things to us," he finally explained. "That was what she said she was doing. On us and our goat. And our dog." He looked down.

"She would speak to you?" Pesdari snapped.

"Sometimes," Capar responded warily.

"What would she say?"

Capar squinted at her face's shadows before he continued.

"That we were going to help her learn how to transport her mind or something."

Despite the fear and confusion reeling in her own mind, Pesdari never stopped moving forward. How long had Thade's tests gone unnoticed? How had *she* not seen what was going on? Death came for all in the end. That was how it should be, no, how it must be, but Thade had been searching for a way to circumvent death. A hiss of realization sliced through Pesdari's teeth. While she could not say that she had a full understanding of Thade's magic, she was sure she understood why Anicen and Capar had been so horrifyingly transfigured. Thade must have been practicing at building a new body, seeing how well she could magically knit odds and ends together. For who knows how long, she had been working on living subjects to test the mettle of her magic. When her friend had become so warped Pesdari didn't know. Had this transformation from friend into fiend happened slowly? Like the twisting of vines around a tree? Digging in tighter and tighter until it was too late?

A sound cut through the darkness. Pesdari's thoughts blinked into silence. Something hard was scraping along stone. The trio froze as the horrible *SCCCREEEEeeeech* echoed throughout the caverns. A mad howl followed it. Anicen began to growl softly, and Capar's eyes went wide.

"There's no time," hissed Pesdari. She began to rush off after the glowing stone trail. The boys followed once again. She thanked the gods that the stones seemed to be leading them away from the noise. They followed the trail in silence as it led them deeper into the cave. Pesdari was the first to see that the stones disappeared into a crevice that ran up a rock wall. She grit her teeth and slid her shoulder into it. Jagged rocks pressed against her spine. The space was so tight she could barely turn her head, but with the limited movement she did have, she could see the faint glimmer of the stones leading onward. She began to inch her way through the crevice.

"I don't want to go in there, Anicen," Capar whispered as he watched Pesdari and their only source of light disappear into the stone wall. His stomach was roiling with hunger, and he was so tired. It felt like they had been running for days. His brother grabbed his horns and shook Capar's head playfully before giving his brother a big lick on the forehead. Capar grinned despite himself. Anicen then wiggled into the crevice after Pesdari and the light; his hand stuck out from the rock as an invitation to his brother.

Capar didn't see his brother's kind gesture in the dark. He crept closer to the wall and squawked as he caught a finger in his eye, but then he gratefully took the hand and slipped inside the crevice too. He moved forward, first an inch, then a few more. He could hear his horns scraping along the rock walls that held him enclosed. Pressing his palms against the wall behind him he tried to move forward again. He remained where he was. He tried again with no success. Capar shattered with panic; his horns were stuck. Capar tried to thrash himself free. He jerked back and forth, but it was no use. He could feel Anicen's hand squeezing his, trying to calm him while simultaneously pulling his arm in an attempt to help him.

"The horns! I'm stuck, Anicen! I'm stuck!"

There was a whine next to him. Anicen understood.

"What are you two doing?" Pesdari snarled. She had already popped out the other side of the narrow passageway and was standing in a wide open cavern that glittered in the dim light emitted by her enchanted burning slippers.

"I'm stuck!" Capar wailed. Anicen's whines had turned to anxious panting. He let go of his brother's hand.

"Don't leave me!" shrieked Capar. "Don't!"

Anicen pushed himself out of the crevice. He immediately grabbed Pesdari by the wrist and pulled her over to the rock wall. She shook him off her.

"Wait!" she snapped. She approached the crevice where Capar was sobbing inside.

"Stop crying. Take a deep breath," she ordered. "We'll get you out."

Peering inside, she could just make out the small boy's form and his horns, wedged tight between the rocks. As the words left her mouth, Pesdari felt a twinge in her gut. The rock wall was immense. While using the vast amount of material here to form a stone object would be easy, trying to widen the crevice could potentially have deadly side effects. She could very well bring the entire wall down upon them if she tried to do this by herself. Anicen impatiently growled behind her. She glared over her shoulder at the cursed figure.

"I'm thinking!" she snarled.

"I don't want to die here," Capar wailed. "I want to go home! I want to go home!"

"You're not going to die," Pesdari said coldly, but her jaw was set tight. The situation was far from ideal.

If Thade had already made her way into the cavernous underbelly of the coven's stronghold, the boy's cries could lead her straight to them. If that were the case, getting Capar out would be the best way to increase her odds of survival, but, on the other hand, his chances of getting out of the crevice, even with her magical aid, were slim. They could all die, and yet, if Thade found them, she would surely kill them all. There was no denying that.

She stared at the sobbing little boy who continued begging her to help him. With an exasperated growl, she made her decision. Her palms flattened on either side of the crevice. Her instinct to survive flooded through her fingertips, as she thought over and over, "*I need you to MOVE!*"

The whole cavern began to fill with a threatening rumble as pebbles and stones started to fall within the crevice. Behind her, Anicen barked furiously. As debris pelted his head, Capar realized there was just enough space for him to slide along the crevice as long as he kept his head facing forward. His heart racing, he moved as quickly as he could through the shuddering rock, tears streaming down his face. The rock wall, stationary for thousands of years, was fighting off Pesdari's magical interventions, and the resulting angry vibrations set his teeth to chattering. He involuntarily bit deep into his tongue and blood filled his mouth. A rock slammed against the top of his head. Stars exploded before his eyes but he continued shuffling forward. At last, he burst into the cavern.

As if enraged that its prey had escaped, the wall roared and large boulders fell from the cavern's ceiling. Capar's exhilaration at escaping his stone tomb quickly transformed into fear again as he watched destruction rain down upon them.

Anicen clutched him close, protectively tucking his little brother's head under his arms. Pesdari's hands were still pressed against the sheet of rock before her. She seemed to be frozen in place. Capar screamed as a massive rock fell just three feet behind him and his brother. A spray of shattered rubble showered them. Still, Pesdari did not move. Anicen shoved Capar toward a rock wall on their right and ran to her. He grabbed her by the waist, yanking her violently away. Debris still continued to fall, but there was an immediate break in the intense vibrations. As Anicen dragged her further from the crevice, a boulder crashed in front of the opening.

The flame still floated above Pesdari's head, and as Capar scurried after his brother to help drag her limp form along the edge of the cavern to avoid being crushed by falling rocks, he realized she had passed out. As rocks continued to fall, Anicen and Capar huddled together with Pesdari beneath them. Slowly, the terrifying crashes ceased. Anicen glanced up, thankful that the light from Pesdari's fire had not been extinguished, but no sooner had the thought crossed his mind, then the slippers were destroyed by one last falling stone. Capar heard his brother sigh. They sat in the darkness, relishing what felt like a pause of the world.

"I can't see. Can yah smell anything?" Capar finally asked Anicen. He listened to his brother tap his finger twice against a rock. After Thade had merged Anicen's face with that of their dog's and stolen his ability to speak, he and his brother had worked up a new form of communication. While Anicen was often tied to the table, and he would be restrained in the other chamber, Anicen's hands still had some freedom. Capar would call out to him, and Anicen would tap on the table to respond. One tap meant 'no,' two meant 'yes'. Desperate for communication and to feel slightly normal again, Capar had even helped his brother construct signals that he could use as insults.

Curious as to what Anicen could be smelling, Capar turned

his head reflexively. His face smashed straight into the rock wall they were huddling against.

"Ow!"

"*Tap—TapTap—Tap*," signaled Anicen.

"I'm not an idiot!" griped Capar as his brother huffed out his strange dog laugh. Suddenly, he felt his brother's hands pressing down on both his shoulders.

"Yah want me to stay here?"

"*TapTap*," Anicen signaled. He stood and cautiously walked forward, his hand against the rock wall so he wouldn't lose his way in the dark. His nose twitched as he sniffed the air. There was certainly something in the cavern. It wasn't alive — that he knew without a doubt. The smell was both familiar and bizarre to him but most smells were these days. While the shock of owning such an impressive olfactory system had worn off, he wasn't sure if he would ever get used to how much more extraordinary scents were to him, especially now that he wasn't locked away. New smells were flooding his nostrils, but he focused on the most profound. It was one that made his mouth water and his stomach grumbled with excitement in the dark. As he moved closer, his nose twitched furiously.

"*It's got to be right here*," he thought to himself. Sticking his hands out in front of him, he felt a pile of rocks. He frowned. This couldn't be right. There was something good here, he knew it. He squatted and began to feel around in the dark. This was driving him mad. Scents were filling his nose, but he kept feeling rocks. His hand touched something coarse. He gripped it tight.

"Anicen?" Capar called out nervously. He jerked in fright as something plopped next to his feet. He calmed when he heard Anicen tap out a message.

"*TapTapTap*." Elation ran through Capar as he translated his brother's message.

"Yah found food!"

His hands stretched out in the inky blackness, feeling for

whatever Anicen had dropped at his feet. As he touched it, he realized that his brother had found some sort of sack. He stuck his hands inside it and pulled something out. Whatever it was smelled good. He tentatively touched his tongue to it, and his senses alerted him that he was tasting a strip of cured meat. He didn't hesitate to bite into it. Anicen was already ripping at his meal. The two boys ate until their stomachs were content. When they were done, Anicen touched Pesdari's shoulder. He shook it slightly, but she didn't move. His hand rested just over her nose. Soft puffs of air hit his skin.

He heard Capar whisper, "Is she dead?"

"*Tap.*"

"What do we do now?" Capar asked. His eyes were adjusting to the darkness, but he felt like he had been swallowed by some monstrous beast. Anicen rubbed his hands against his face. His lips stretched wide as he yawned. He tried to get comfortable and leaned his head back against the rock wall. Pesdari lay beside him on his right. He hoped they would stay warm until she woke up. They needed to keep moving, but he was sure without her, he and Capar would never find their way out.

"*TapTap—Tap,*" he played on a rock next to him.

"Do yah think it's safe to sleep here?" Capar worried.

"*TapTap—Tap.*"

"Ok, ok," Capar muttered as he curled up on the cold ground, his back to Pesdari. Anicen reached across Pesdari's prone body and felt his brother's shirt. He pulled the younger boy closer to the unconscious figure. Capar didn't put up a fight. He was too tired, and he realized that he actually felt a little bit warmer. Soon, Anicen heard his brother's breath relax, and then he too drifted off to sleep.

Chapter 9
The Gods

Pesdari did not wake up peacefully. Her consciousness was launched back into the world of the living. Bolting upright in the black void of the cavern, her panic quelled as she felt the weight of the boys' sleeping bodies pressed against her legs. She wiggled a foot experimentally.

"*So,*" she thought with a tight lipped grin. "*I survived.*"

She couldn't help but groan as she drew her knees up and rested her arms on them, her hands dangling. While the cavern was quiet and still, her body was loud with a multitude of grievances. Her fingers twitched involuntarily, her muscles flared with discomfort, and she had a splitting headache. Yet, even though the act of sitting was a strain on her delirious body, she was very much alive and grateful for it.

"*I shouldn't have been able to do that,*" Pesdari mused while rolling her stiff neck. She still couldn't believe that she had attempted such a mad thing for two strangers who were sure to be nothing but a burden to her. She shook her head at her foolishness and immediately regretted the action as a wave of nausea swept through her.

"Breathe, just breathe," she whispered to herself, forcing her lungs to expel air and then fill in a slow, controlled manner. Well, she considered with a sigh as her stomach calmed its protests, it had been a mad day, and she had seen acts of magic performed that she had never even thought possible. She supposed that in the hectic whirlwind of their escape from Thade's wrath, her mind had gone into a sort of frenzy of its own. She promised herself she would not commit such rash, destructive acts again.

One of the boys groaned in his sleep. Pesdari turned her head, but the darkness that enveloped her was so severe she couldn't see a thing. Her addled mind was perturbed at her lack of vision. Where were her slippers? Surely they could provide some light. She realized with a grimace that they must have been destroyed while she was unconscious.

"Wonderful," she grumbled. "Now I'm blind and barefoot."

There was nothing else to do but lie back down on the ground. From her place of rest, she idly wondered if they would be trapped in this cavern forever. She had no idea what had followed after she had worked her magic. There were only fragments of memory that sparked in her mind, but before a haze of shrieking muscles and a horrific stabbing behind her eyes had swallowed her world, she remembered seeing Capar moving closer through the crevice as rocks had showered down around her. Their eyes had met for just a moment before hers had rolled back in her head, and Hetra's earthquake voice had consumed her.

"Death in all things, little one. Death in all things, but not for you three. Not yet."

Her vision had been flooded then with sheets of rock surging upwards through watery depths. She stood as a mountain peak defying the screaming of the winds before she was transformed into waves of stone and dirt that crushed trees and all the beasts that were too slow to escape the path of her destruction. She had become an avalanche bearing down on all creation, and it did not matter, because she was of the earth and all that she consumed was of her as well. They became one in death, one in life. Blood, bones, and rock all became crushed together in a tragic, everlasting existence. She remembered that she had throbbed with pain and despair, but there had also been a bizarre sense of peace. Pesdari removed herself from her memories and furrowed her brows.

"No, not peace," she realized. *"Completion."*

She touched her chilled hands together as she mulled over the vision but paused when she felt small, hard lumps in her palms. Even without a light Pesdari knew exactly what they were. Pieces of the rock wall were ingrained under her skin. Rolling her thumb over them, she assumed that the crevice had widened for her because Hetra had assisted in the gargantuan task by making her a part of the underground cavern itself. Through this connection alone she had been able to save Capar and stay alive while performing her magical feat. A thought struck her. Pesdari placed her left palm flat against the ground and tentatively commanded, "Rise."

To her surprise, there was a terrific grumble and a fierce cracking sound as a stone pillar suddenly shot up from the cavern floor just where Anicen was curled up, asleep. The abrupt emergence of this new rock formation sent him tumbling with a yelp. Pesdari was frozen with shock as she heard stone dislodge itself. Pebbles dropped from on high, so she raised her arm to shielded herself. Capar cried out next, and the sound brought Pesdari back to herself. She pulled back her hand and held it close to her chest. The pillar stopped growing. Pesdari put out her hand to touch her newly created rock formation, and her mouth opened in awe. More power than she ever thought possible thrummed through her. It frightened her so much that she began to claw at the small bits of stone embedded in her palms. She had wanted to escape this place and its gods — not become one of their greatest students. A freezing rush of air flowed over her. Her skin grew cold. Pesdari was locked in place, petrified.

"Be sttttttiiiiiilll, be stttiiiiiiiillllll," hissed a voice of winds and gales in her ear. Pesdari made to scream but choked on her own spit.

"The onnnneee still folllooooowwsss. Accept our bllleeeeesssingsss," she heard Egal command between her hacking coughs. Smoke began to fill her nostrils, and it raced against Pesdari's terror towards her heart. She wasn't sure which would be the victor.

"We have chosen you, little ember! We have a task for you," hissed Riefon with a hideous laugh that sliced through Pesdari's brain.

"No, no, no," she whispered with the fervor of prayer. She clutched her head. "I don't want your blessings, I don't want your tasks — leave me alone!"

A snarl snapped like a whip in her mind.

"WHAT!"

It sounded like someone was right behind her; however, Pesdari knew better than to turn around. She was sure this was all happening in her head, but when the cavern erupted into flames and the stone floor melted into lava that swirled near her feet, her certainty was shaken. She heard Riefon's voice again. It echoed in the now fiery room.

"What was that, you lump of coal?"

Pesdari's mouth went dry as a skeleton draped in purple robes emerged from the lava. The heat was nigh unbearable, but she couldn't tear her eyes away from the awesome sight before her. The bones that now levitated above the magma were as black as night. Even though there was no flesh to speak of, Pesdari was sure the empty eye sockets were enraged and glaring at her. The skull, as well as the rest of the bones, was lined with fractures. Bone fragments seemed to shift before Pesdari's eyes as she realized that molten lava flowed underneath the bones. The edges of the beautiful fabric the skeleton wore dipped into the pool of lava below and curled as they burned, but the flame never spread further than the cloth's hem.

Pesdari's mouth mirrored that of a fish as she bore witness to the magnificence of Riefon, the god of fire. The god crooked a bony finger at her. Terrified, she inched closer to the edge of the rock that was still untouched by the fiery lake before her. The intensity of the heat made her shield her face.

"There is life. There is death. Always will the two meet."

Riefon paused before looking away from Pesdari and sighed, "My raging spark, my brave fire, she burns too bright. She wishes to burn forever, but it cannot be. She has lost her way."

Turning back to look at her, the god pointed a finger. Pesdari wasn't sure if it was just the shadows, but the skull seemed to have furrowed its brows so it could glower reproachfully at her.

"There must be death in all things. You will complete Thade's circle," Riefon commanded.

"Please, I barely escaped her!" she cried. Riefon said nothing. Black smoke billowed out from the god's robes. With almost fiendish delight, it swirled up Pesdari's nose and down her throat.

"You are of the coven! It is your duty to protect these natural laws!" Riefon roared as she gagged and struggled for air. "You-"

"-Mercy, Riefon, show her mercy," a cool voice interrupted. Riefon glanced back with an air of annoyance but still gripped the robes to give them a quick shake. The smoke dispersed. Pesdari inhaled sharply as her airways became clear, but now spouts of steam were sizzling all around her. The lake of fire had been split down the middle. One side continued to burn as the other lapped with gentle waves of deep blue water. As Pesdari hacked up violent coughs, a pair of bright yellow eyes looked down on her. She stared back in shock.

Tewar, the god of water, was standing over her. The god's smooth eel skin rippled in the light cast by Reifon's fire. While the god moved with no apparent difficulty, huge chunks of flesh seemed to have been bitten away and numerous fishing hooks had sunk in deep to the god's ribs. Pesdari could even see barbed tips emerging through one of the god's cheeks. Blood drifted up and away from the wounds as if the god were still swimming far below in the watery depths of his realm. Sharp teeth smiled down upon the hapless mortal. She looked away in reverence.

"No creature can live forever," Tewar intoned, but then in a softer voice requested, "Look upon me, Pesdari."

A slimy, cold hand raised Pesdari's chin so she could gaze once more upon the awesome and terrible god.

"We are life and death incarnate, for without one the other cannot be," Tewar gestured to the hooks and bite marks. "This circle is eternal. It must never be broken."

"I am not powerful enough to kill her," Pesdari protested in a whisper, desperate for these supreme beings to understand that she was not like them. She was capable, of course, and smart, but the things that she had seen Thade do were so far beyond her comprehension that her spirit recoiled at the thought of coming close to her again; she knew that facing down Thade meant facing down certain death.

"Of course, you're not. She is an inferno, and you are candlelight," Riefon sneered. Pesdari was shocked at the sudden burst of almost petty annoyance she felt. She had always known that Thade had been particularly devoted to her studies of fire, but she hadn't realized just how dedicated her once-upon-a-time friend had been to the god. Clearly, Riefon's affection for Thade was mutual, but Pesdari found this outpouring of affection incredibly irritating.

"We call upon you, Pesdari," Tewar spoke again. "Soon you will be the only one of your kind that can stop her."

Pesdari's eyes went wide.

"What?" she gasped. Her hair swirled in front of her face as someone whispered, "They are dyyyyinng. They are aaaaalll dyyyinng."

She turned and gaped as she looked directly into the gaunt face of Egal. There were no eyes to stare at in horror, only flesh filled sockets and shredded lips that parted in ragged breaths. The god of air had no human nose, but two diagonal slits flared rhythmically. A bright red rash stretched from Egal's chin to the right eye socket, and the god shuddered with feverish energy. Long, white hair whipped all around Pesdari; she felt as if she had stepped into a storm, and yet, there was no familiar screaming of wind in the air. All was quiet — except for the drumming of her heart.

"Soooon they will all be gone," Egal told her. Pesdari tried her best not to gag at the foul scented air rushing against her.

"Her feeeeeaaaast is teeeeerrible."

Pesdari couldn't help herself. She scrambled away from Egal and pressed her back to the cavern wall. Her fists pushed hard against her eyes. This heinous meeting must end; she wasn't sure how much more she could endure.

"Little one, there is no one else to ask," someone rumbled directly behind her. Pesdari turned on her heel to see something that looked like a man but clearly wasn't a man stepping out from the stone wall. Hetra, the god of earth, with a moss and mud covered body that anchored all manner of fungi, loomed over her. A hand that was rough like bark rested on the top of her head.

"We will give you a blessing to strengthen you. Now that the cave rests within you, you will find your way to our forest," Hetra told her. The mushrooms protruding where the god's eyes should have been, glowed.

"Find the Dowhas, and speak these words. As it is in nature, as it is with the gods, let it be so with you," Tewar said. A breezy, "Killlll heeerrrrr," flew from Egal's lips.

"Yes. Send my spark to me," barked Riefon. A wheel of fire rose up and began to slowly turn behind the god. He pointed to it.

"Do not let the circle be broken," he commanded.

"What are the Dowhas? I don't-I can't do this!" Pesdari cried out before shrieking as a boom of thunder shook the cavern.

"You promised us any task if the stones were lit for you. We kept our side of the bargain. Now, you must keep yours," Hetra rumbled.

Fearsome bolts of lightning cracked along the stone ceiling. Their searing light cast foreboding shadows on the gods' faces as each receded from the young woman huddled on the stone floor. With her eyes sealed in terror and her hands clutched protectively over her head, Pesdari was shrouded in darkness. Then, there was silence.

She awoke curled up on her side. The boys snored on either side of her. Leaping to her feet, Pesdari felt for where the pillar had stood. She kicked Anicen in the process, and the boy growled. Pesdari's stomach lurched. The pillar wasn't there. She touched the fingers of her right hand to her left palm, and she fought back the urge to vomit. The small pieces of the cave were still embedded deep within her flesh.

Chapter 10
The Tunnels

Capar snorted himself awake as a hand grabbed his shirt and yanked him to his feet.

"What's going on?" he spluttered.

"Wake up," ordered Pesdari, her voice flat. "It's time to go."

Capar blinked, still half asleep. He could hear his brother yawning and stretching. Capar languidly scratched himself.

"Pe, um, what's yer name again?"

"Pesdari," responded the young woman curtly.

"We found food, Pesdari. D'yah want some?"

Pesdari's stomach growled. She was very hungry. The thought of eating nearly brought a smile to her face. With the supplies she had been promised in hand, it would make their escape from the caves that much easier.

"Yes. Give it to me."

Capar reached out in his brother's general direction, requesting that he share their food. Fully awake now, Anicen gripped the sack tight, wondering if it was wise to reduce their food stores for a moment before slipping his hand inside. He withdrew a bit of dried meat and moved slowly with one of his hands out before him. When he felt Pesdari's eager fingers, he pressed the meat into her waiting palm. She wasted no time sinking her teeth into it. He could hear her savage chewing, and the scent of her saliva softening the meat made his own mouth water.

His nose twitched at the scents swirling around him; he began to drool with desire. His human wits snapped him out of his reverie. Mortified, he quickly wiped his lips dry with the back of his arm. The slightly drooping lips of his canine mouth dragged along his skin. Strong, pointed teeth pressed against his wrist. A sickly flower of shame blossomed within him. Anicen was glad of the dark. He was glad that he could hide his cursed face. A new demand from Pesdari cut his thoughts short.

"Give me more."

He reached back into the sack and withdrew the last piece of meat. Pesdari scarfed it down with gusto.

"What else did you find?" she asked the boys. Anicen sighed as he handed her the empty bag. Pesdari recognized the texture of the bag, but as she felt around for its contents a scowl marred her features.

"That was all there was?" she snapped.

Capar was quiet, not wishing to be a target for her anger. He had seen the rage that could possess these people of the forest. The damaging power they wielded had been used on him many times. His muscles tensed as Anicen grunted. Pesdari growled irritably but did nothing more.

"At least this sack can be useful," he heard her mutter. Soon after, the sack was burning above their heads, illuminating the destruction around them. Capar stared at the massive boulders that now stood throughout the cavernous space. Once an open room, it was now a maze. His heart sank. They would never get out of here, he thought to himself. He would die without ever seeing his village again. Glancing over at his brother, Capar noticed tears glittering in the older boy's eyes. He moved closer to him and gripped his hand. Anicen blinked away his tears and squeezed his brother's fingers. The older boy was glad that Pesdari wasn't looking at him. She was concentrating on the stone walls.

Her fingers gently traced along the grooves and ridges of the rock. She looked over her shoulder and frowned. Like her, neither of the boys had any kind of protection for their feet. Although her skin was buzzing with the whispers of the cave and its caverns as she touched the wall, her mind drew her back to more practical things. Walking through this underground labyrinth was dangerous enough without having to worry about them all slicing open their feet on jagged stones.

"Come here," she ordered. The boys cautiously moved closer to her.

"Sit down." The pair did as instructed, but Anicen's eyes glared at her in suspicion. She balefully looked at him.

"I'm not going to hurt you. Stop looking at me like that."

She knelt before them and began scooping pebbles together in her hands. She took Capar's bare, dirty feet and began to rub the stones against his toes, arches, and heels. His skin tickled and itched.

"What are yah doing!"

"Hardening your soles so you don't get cut," Pesdari told him, irritably.

"*Another thing I never would have known how to do before*," she mused to herself. Her movements were so precise though, it felt as if she had practiced this skill for years.

"*The wonders of the gods*," she thought bitterly.

Capar wriggled as his skin began to produce calluses that they hadn't earned. He froze when Pesdari snapped, "Stop squirming!"

When she finished administering her magic, Capar hopped up and took a few steps away from her as she began to give Anicen's feet the same treatment. The boys touched their feet in wonder as Pesdari turned her attention to her own feet. Then she rose and stared down at them both.

"Follow me."

She led them around the boulders silently, her hand never leaving the rock wall. As she moved, she could sense the turning of the tunnels. Paths that twisted further into the cold sent shivers through her, but there was a glimmer of warmth in the rock. The smallest tremor of hope. Pesdari followed the tremor, desperate for it to lead her to safety. The flaming sack burning above them cast eerie shadows that made Capar squeak with fear from time to time, but it seemed that the quiet trio were the only ones present in the winding space. They walked for hours until Pesdari suddenly stopped. Unceremoniously, she slid to the ground and curled onto her side.

"I'm tired," she announced. Ancien sat down a few feet away from her, watching till she fell asleep. Sure she wasn't faking her rest, Anicen poked his brother in the ribs and held a finger to his lips. Capar stared as his older brother reached under his shirt to reveal a small pouch hanging around his neck. Anicen took it off and opened it. Strips of dried meat where stuffed inside. Capar reached out, but Anicen cinched the pouch closed and put it back around his neck.

"Later?" Capar whispered, hopeful.

"*Tap*," Anicen responded, then jerked his head to the right. His nose twitched. There was a faint smell drifting through the air. He couldn't place it, but his lips curled instinctively. Capar stared in the direction of his brother's snarling muzzling.

"What is it?" the younger boy whispered fearfully. Anicen's brows furrowed before he shook his head. He waved off his momentary defensiveness and gestured for his brother to rest beside him. Cold and hunger were no match for their weariness. Exhausted, they fell into a deep sleep and dreamed of home.

...

The village was burning. Anicen was frozen as he watched his parents roast under the hands of the wicked one. Thade was a surrounded by a fiery sphere that was consuming in the village.

"No! No!" he screamed, but the one who had cursed him just laughed as she showed him her hands covered in his parents' ashes.

Whimpering, Anicen awoke to darkness. The sack had burned out while they slept. He tried to calm himself by whispering a silly saying his father had taught him, but the only sound that came was a strange grunting. Anicen brought a hand to his muzzle.

"*It's not even my muzzle*," Anicen thought bitterly. Small, unnatural snuffing sounds were lost in the tunnel as the boy mourned for himself and his dog. Time passed. It could have been minutes or hours, Anicen wasn't sure. All he knew was that he couldn't stand another moment alone in this abysmal place.

He approached where he thought Pesdari was sleeping and kicked out, making contact with her foot. She woke with a start but quickly regained her composure.

"The sack is gone," she said to herself before dragging her aching body upright, automatically putting her hand out to the wall.

"Wake your brother," she said and began to walk. Without the light of the sack, the wanderers slammed their toes into rocks and the protuding edges of the wall cut at their legs. Capar was crying as he followed the older members of his party. He was tired and beginning to think there was no end to this tunnel. They would just keep walking and walking forever. He longed so much for his family and his friends in the village; he couldn't contain his loss. Quietly, the young boy began to sing a little lullaby to himself about a hunter who rose with the sun. The hunter chased his prey all through the day, but when the night would come, the hunter would come home and watch over all the snoring little ones.

Pesdari's body locked. Her hand still on the stone wall, she cocked her head to the side. Echoes of a man's soft voice floated through her mind in the same tune the boy now sang. It was a sound as familiar as air but just as impossible to grab hold of.

"I-I know that song…"

"Yah do?"

"Mm. The words are... wrong though..."

"No, they're not!" Capar retorted, his sadness interrupted by indignation.

"Yes, they are," Pesdari replied with confidence.

"How would do you know?"

"I must have heard it before coming to the Coven."

Capar scrambled a little closer. Now, this was interesting news.

"Yah weren't grown like a tree?" he asked her. He had Anicen had come up with many theories about the people who lived in this awful place. He wanted to know if his theory was correct. Pesdari couldn't hold back a laugh.

"No. I was born outside. My mother was killed, and I was brought here," she explained.

"Did they kill yer ma?" he questioned her. Pesdari frowned.

"No. They didn't."

"Huh. Well, where were yah born!" Capar demanded. He was invigorated by this strange information.

"I don't know."

"What was your family's name?"

"I don't know what that means."

"What!"

"We don't have that in the Coven. I don't know what it means."

"It's yer family's name!" Capar exclaimed, shocked at Pesdari's stupidity. "That's how you know who's in your family."

"I see."

"Ours is Fylaim. Capar and Anicen Fylaim!"

"Oh."

"So how's your song go? The one that's *actually* wrong?" Capar asked. Pesdari took a breath. Something about this song set her teeth on edge and stung her eyes. The tune matched Capar's, but in her lullaby, the hunter rose at night to fend off dark dreams. The hunter lit up every star to scare beasts away from sleeping children.

Anicen raised his eyebrows, surprised. At first he had been as incredulous as Capar when Pesdari made her corrections, but then he remembered. When the fishermen would come from the big town they would sometimes sing the song just as Pesdari had.

"*How does she know that*?" he wondered, and then he heard Capar laugh.

"Yer a terrible singer."

"I don't sing much."

"Obviously," Capar snickered. Anicen huffed his dog laugh. It had been a long time since he'd heard his little brother sound happy. Reaching into the pouch around his neck, he brought out a piece of meat. He was about to hand it to Capar but paused. With a sigh, he tapped Pesdari's shoulder.

"Wha-unf!" Pesdari had turned her face directly into Anicen's outstretched hand and caught a knuckle to the eye.

"What are you doing?" she snapped. Anicen grumbled an apology that no one could understand and felt for her hand. He gave her the meat.

Pesdari paused.

"*He was hiding this*," she thought. Her empty stomach twinged with anger, but she quickly calmed herself with a bite of the food. Of course, he had been hiding it. Only an idiot would share rations with someone they were planning on killing after they had outlived their usefulness. Pesdari listened to the two boys comforting and caring for each other in the blackness. She snorted.

"*They won't kill me*," she thought. They were not like the children she had grown up with. The pair of them had saved her from Thade instead of abandoning her. She stopped herself before she ate all of the strip.

"Little one. C-Capar. Come here," she said, faltering in her attempt to be gentle. She heard him shuffle up to her. She reached out in the dark for his hand, and when she touched him he twitched but didn't pull away. She placed the remaining meat in his palm.

"Eat this," she told him. There was quiet in the tunnel before Capar said in small voice, "Thank yah, Pesdari."

She grunted, and they moved further into the waiting cavern.

Chapter 11

The Forest

Three tongues pressed themselves against the tunnel's wall, desperate for a drink. If luck were with them, they would find a cool trickle of water running down, but nearly every time they searched, their only reward was a damp stone. Pesdari tried not to dwell on it. She knew it had been a dangerously long time since she had last quenched her thirst.

"Tewar is worthy of worship," she groaned as she sucked on her tongue.

"Who's Tewar?" Capar asked. For a moment, Pesdari forgot that Capar was not a child of the coven and opened her mouth to chastise his impertinence.

"Watch your tong-oh. Yes. You don't know the old gods, do you?"

It was not a question.

"I do too!" he chirped, offended somewhere behind Pesdari.

"Oh?"

"The old women back home always said Riefon would play tricks and stoke the flames too much so their soup would boil over."

Pesdari snorted with amusement, greatly enjoying the god's demotion to an impish trickster.

"Yes, Riefon is a bother at times," she replied. Encouraged,

Capar happily chattered on about the gods and their ways, getting almost everything about them wrong. A few things he said even made Pesdari laugh. Just as Capar was about to launch on an explanation of why the god of water's name was Temars, *not* Tewar, she stopped. The brothers heard her whispering feverishly before she announced, "It's close. The end is close!"

Tears erupted from Anicen's eyes, and he joyfully tugged on his brother's horns. Capar tried to contain a squeal of delight but failed miserably. His happy exclamation earned him a stern rebuke to be quiet from Pesdari; he didn't care. Powered by renewed vigor, they all continued on. They hadn't walked much deeper into the tunnel before Anicen began to growl. The low guttural sound turned Pesdari's stomach to ice despite recognizing its source.

"Something is ahead?" she whispered.

TapTap.

"That means yes," Capar whimpered. Pesdari didn't even have a moment to curse before a chittering noise traveled down the tunnel. It was coming closer very quickly. Capar screamed as two red eyes blinked at them before rising higher into the air.

Pesdari's mind went white with panic. Her body was painfully weak. She was hungry and tired. There was barely any energy left within her to conduct magic, but her freedom was so close. Her lips drew back. She and Anicen stood together with their teeth bared before she let loose a wild scream. A gale rushed from her throat. It ripped through the passage, knocking loose rocks from their places. The approaching creature was thrown against an opposing wall. Capar's hands were clapped to his ears as the piercing scream continued. Then, there was silence, and Pesdari sank to her knees. Anicen rushed toward the fallen creature, his nose guiding him. He stepped on part it. Instinct overwhelmed him as he lunged, fangs searching for their prize. A shriek quickly turned into a gurgle. Anicen was again thankful for the darkness as he returned, panting. Warm blood soaked his face. The taste was buzzing in his head. He swiped his arms against his muzzle. He didn't want Capar to ever see him like this.

"Anicen," croaked Pesdari. Her throat was so raw, her voice could barely squeeze out. Cautiously stepping forward, he found her and pulled her up.

"Keep... walking," she gasped. Her feet scrambled under her as her head drooped. Only Anicen's tight grasp kept her upright. Capar gripped the back of his brother's ragged shirt, but the older boy shrugged him off. The thing in the dark had been large. He needed to be able to move quickly if another one appeared. Anicen hadn't been able to see much of the creature, but he had gotten lucky. His fangs had sunk into its throat on his first bite. The throat had been wide, and the frame he had held onto muscular. Without Pesdari's magic, they would have all been killed; he was sure of it. Nose twitching furiously, the three struggled as fast as they could through the passage.

Capar blinked. Something brushed his cheek that he hadn't felt in a long, long time. A smile overtook his dirty face.

"A breeze!" he squealed. He ran past his brother and Pesdari. He slipped, scraping his leg badly, but he was up in an instant. Anicen barked after him and tried to keep up as Pesdari croaked, "Stop! Stop!"

The little boy's happiness superseded his caution as he flung himself with abandon after the breeze. This must be the way out, he just knew it. Then he saw a dusky, lavender light twinkling ahead of him. Capar whooped and ran as fast as he could. Clambering over a large rock that blocked the path, he was at last at the mouth of the tunnel. An opening that would have just been big enough for his father to squeeze through stood before him. Smells of trees and grass swept over him. Without thinking, Capar rushed out of the tunnel. Staggering forward he collapsed into the soft grass that looked silver in the twilight. The sight rooted him to the spot. He had thought that he would never see grass again. He began to weep.

Anicen lowered Pesdari to the ground next to his brother. He could hardly believe his eyes. He stared at the black trees surrounding them and looked back at the tunnel. They had made it. They had survived. He took a few steps back toward the opening of the tunnel to make sure nothing else from inside was following them. Something rumbled. A pile of rocks began to quake. Anicen took a step closer for a better view, fascinated and horrified. As he did so, the rocks began to move. One rolled onto another to form shoulders, arms, and legs. Suddenly, a living rock statue loomed before him. The monstrosity didn't have eyes, but it lurched toward Anicen all the same. He began to bark as Capar screamed. Pesdari, pale and sweating, tried to crawl away.

"A... guardian," she hacked out. "Run!"

The younger boy began to drag her by the shoulders. Anicen ran to them and forced Pesdari to her feet. The monster began to throw large rocks at their fleeing heels. The only way to escape was to run deeper into Yrecep Forest, and so, the trio ran.

...

Their feet hadn't carried them too great a distance, but they were far enough away from the rock monster to rest. Panting, Anicen slumped against the black trunk of a tree. He was desperate for water. He surveyed his companions. Capar was curled up on his side, intermittently crying and yawning. Pesdari was reclining against her own tree trunk. Her skin looked waxy, and her eyes stared into nothing.

"What was that?" Capar sniffled. Pesdari blinked languidly at him.

"A guardian. To keep intruders from coming into the coven."

"Who would want to go there?"

Pesdari shook her head in answer. The pair fell into silence.

Anicen's brow was furrowed as he watched them. He had to find water. Every fiber in his being wanted to run as far he could from the coven, but he had been lost in Yrecep Forest once before. He knew he needed to proceed with caution as he had back all that time ago.

"*And look what that got yah,*" he thought ruefully. He hadn't been cautious enough to be suspicious of a woman wandering in the forest, in *this* forest. He had accepted the woman's gifts of water and food and got he and his brother kidnapped. Clenching his fist, he took a breath to calm himself. Then, he crouched down and made gestures of 'stay' and 'drink' to his brother, who nodded. As Anicen walked through the silver grass, he glanced over his shoulder. Pesdari was staring after him. She almost looked dead. He huffed and hardened his resolve. He had to find water. Without her magic, they would all die. He knew it. Then, the black trees swallowed him, and he disappeared from Pesdari's sight.

Anicen thanked every spirit and god he could think of when he found the stream. The water moved slowly by the sides of two sloping banks peppered with indigo flowers. Anicen thrust his muzzle into the water and began to drink. On the other side of the bank, dark figures watched him. The figures glided from tree to tree, melding into the black, smooth bark. Unblinking eyes bore holes into the back of Anicen's head, but he could not smell these interlopers. There was nothing to smell or bite — only shadow and dull, milky eyes.

Chapter 12
The Dowhas

With his thirst quenched, Anicen was actually beginning to feel hopeful. Once he brought his brother and Pesdari to the stream, things would be alright for them. There were enough fallen branches around to build a shelter, and after Pesdari had a drink, she could start a fire for them, he thought. Anicen then stuck his nose in the air for a cursory sniff that sent his brain popping with scents. His tongue peeked between his lips, and his stomach gleefully rumbled. There were certainly things worth eating in the forest. If he found the right materials, he could try to build a trap. At the thought of catching prey, his tongue lolled happily. Legs bouncing, he started back to his companions. He never realized he was being stalked.

Shadowy figures moved without a sound after him. More and more joined the hunt, blocking out the evening light. Anicen noticed the gathering dark but thought nothing of it. He poked this head around a tree, panting with satisfaction at the sight of his companions. Capar was chewing on a piece of grass, looking bored. Pesdari was asleep. Anicen yipped cheerfully and waved. Capar hopped to his feet as his brother gently shook Pesdari by the shoulder. When she opened her eyes, he was heartened to see that they were a little clearer. Anicen's good mood was short lived though. A pitiful moan rose behind him.

"Anicen... something's here," Capar said. Glancing back at his brother, Anicen saw that a ring of impenetrable night had formed around them. Yanking Capar behind him, Anicen began snarling and snapping at the miasma of shadow bearing down upon them. While the dark mass seemed to be one enormous wall, there were strange shapes that marked unique forms within. Tall antlers rose high above one or two heads and a few enormous wings stretched wide, presumably from other creatures' backs. Black as night and silent as the grave, the terrifying figures came closer, threatening to swallow the terrified trio. An incredible pressure suddenly bore down on their chests, as if a boulder had been dropped on them. Capar and Anicen's eyes bulged, gagging for air. The ring grew tighter and tighter, till Pesdari could just begin to make out the faintest details in the shadowy beings' faces. Anguished tears squeezed out of her eyes.

"As it is in nature, as it is with the gods, let it be so with you," Pesdari declared as loudly as she could. Her voice was barely more than a whisper. In an instant, the pressure vanished. All three humans fell to their hands and knees, violently filling their lungs with air.

"The Dowhas will make it so," a chorus of listless voices responded. One shadow separated itself from the rest and bent so its pupil-less eyes gazed into Pesdari's.

"Coven...?" the shadow asked her, its voice a mixture of hisses and whispers. Elongated ears crowned its head.

"Yes. Yes, I'm of the coven," she answered, digging her fingers into the soft dirt. Still doubled over, the shadow turned its head, and the neck stretched until its face was aligned with what would have been the place of a human hip. It stared at the brothers.

"They are of the coven too!" Pesdari lied quickly. The head snapped soundlessly back into place as if it had never moved at all. Nausea gripped her as the Dowhas looked unflinchingly at her. She couldn't tell if it recognized her falsehood or not.

"*We're on the knife's edge of food or friend*," she realized. Then a memory of Thade came to her. Little Thade bossing around older children who had come to take some silly trinket of theirs. Pesdari couldn't remember what but she did remember Thade puffing out her chest and boldly lying that the coven leaders had personally given her the trinket and that if they tried to take it, they would be sorry. Pesdari puffed out her chest and folded her arms just as little Thade had done.

"The gods command me. You must help us," she ordered, hoping that these strange beings wouldn't sense her false bravado. After a moment, the shadow straightened itself.

"Follow," it said. En mass, the Dowhas moved back the way Anican had come.

"*Thank you, Thade*," Pesdari thought wryly. Coughing and terrified, the boys quickly came to her side. Capar turned to her, fearful questions ready to tumble out of his mouth.

"What-"

"-I don't know," Pesdari said through gritted teeth as she uneasily rose to her feet. "All I know is that they are called the Dowhas and that the gods told me to speak to them."

Anicen and Capar exchanged a shocked looked.

"*The gods told her?*" Anicen thought. If he hadn't been trapped so long in the bowels of the coven, he would have assumed that Pesdari was crazy. He had seen awesome and terrible sights in his short life though. Such awesome and terrible sights that he could accept Pesdari's relationship with the gods.

At last, they reached the stream with their strange, silent entourage. Cautiously, the three travelers drank, all rather unnerved to have the Dowhas at their backs. Four dead tibarbs were waiting for them when they finished. The tibarbs' long black ears had white tufts that matched their unfurled fluffy tails. Tibarb could leap tremendous heights and almost fly from tree to tree, collecting nuts they would bring back to their burrows. Every so often one or two would perch on the trees surrounding the Yard. Hungry younglings would take aim with magically infused rocks, and whoever did bring one down would be regaled a hero for giving everyone something other than aseloni meat to eat.

The boys started, dumbfounded, at the game. They had only been at the stream for a few minutes. What could hunt so quickly? Anicen blinked, completely unsure of what to think. Pesdari stood, glaring at the mysterious servants of the gods suspiciously. The group of Dowhas had splintered, but the trio was still surrounded.

"What do we do?" Capar whispered. Anicen growled softly.

"We eat, and we rest," Pesdari told them.

"Will they hurt us?"

"They shouldn't... for now."

Pesdari nearly leaped out of her skin as something bumped against her hip. Capar was leaning against her, trembling. Was he frightened or just cold, she wondered. Frowning, she gently patted his hair. It was filthy, caked with dirt and dust. She plucked out a leaf that had become trapped within his curls. Taking him by a horn, she angled his face to look at her.

"I will watch them," she said to him solemnly. "Now, go gather kindling."

Capar's eyes slid over the remaining Dowhas, but he nodded. Before he inched away from her, Pesdari realized he had stopped trembling. Luckily, plenty of sticks surrounded the fallen branches Anicen had spotted earlier so little Capar didn't have to wander out of sight. Pesdari moved to the edge of the stream, peering down at her feet. Anicen watched her retrieve something from the ground. She walked over to him with a relatively flat stone that was a long as her hand and another in her left. Then, she began to slide the flat stone along the second. Sparks flew. Within minutes, the flat stone had been transformed into a roughly crafted knife. She handed it to Anicen, who cocked his head in wonder.

"Hetra's blades," she said casually, trying to disguise the

exhaustion descending upon her.

"Start work on the tibarbs," she snapped as her legs swayed beneath her. She sat then, refusing to take her eyes off the gliding Dowhas. Uneasily, Anicen turned his attention to his own task. It had been a long time since Anicen had skinned a tibarb with his parents, but the movements came back automatically. He couldn't see any wounds on the animal, and its neck wasn't broken. It was as if it had simply dropped dead.

Capar had dutifully collected an array of sticks and tried his best to arrange them properly for a cooking fire. Pesdari moved toward the pile, running her finger along a stick that looked particularly dry. She grit her teeth as a flame ran from her finger and struck up an acquaintance with the stick. In no time, the flames and the kindling were getting along like a house on fire. Pesdari sucked on her singed finger. She had been too tired to properly protect herself from Riefon's magic. The boys assembled a rudimentary spit and with a few minor setbacks had two of the tibarbs roasting. Night had finally settled upon them, but the group knew that the Dowhas hadn't left.

It was a pleasure to eat fresh meat, and all four tibarb ended up being consumed, no matter how uncomfortable the trio felt to have eyes on them in the dark. Anicen's body begged for sleep, but the cold night air reminded him to build a shelter. Slowly he rose to his feet and began dragging a large branch towards the fire. Pesdari furrowed her brow.

"That is too large for the fire. The knife won't be able to cut through that."

Anicen shook his head and put his fingertips together like the shape of a house. Pesdari's lips pursed in confusion.

"What?"

Anicen huffed and tried to draw his intent in the dirt. Capar was beginning to droop, but came to with a snort as his older brother shook him.

"Wha-what's going on?" the little boy yawned. Anicen pointed to his rough sketch. Rubbing his eyes, Capar looked it over.

"Why didja wake me up to show me a stupid house," he pouted. Pesdari looked over the little boy's shoulder.

"What's a house?" she asked. Anicen huffed irritably before stomping off to drag another branch back. Capar look at her, his shock at her stupidly written on his face.

"It's where you sleep," he said in a highly insulting tone. Before Pesdari could any kind of retribution on his younger brother, Anicen took her by the arm and had her hold the first branch vertically. He had a terrible time trying to communicate that he wanted her to lean his branch against hers, and Capar was no help at all. The little boy was laughing himself silly watching his brother's increasingly wild arm flapping while Pesdari stared in utter confusion. After much struggling, a small lean-to had been erected with one of its entrances facing the fire. Capar was just about to crawl inside when Anicen demonstrated in no uncertain terms that he wasn't getting inside until he contributed. Pouting, the little boy hurriedly gathered leaves and grass to make soft beds for them all. The three of them lay in close quarters but the fire and their body heat made their ramshackle accommodations quite snug. Pesdari closed her eyes with relish. Anicen was already snoring. Next to her, Capar made little sniffling noises.

"What is it?" she asked sharply.

"I'm scared," he whispered. Pesdari sucked in air through her nose, calming herself.

"If you go to sleep you won't be scared," she replied.

"But I can't sleep!" he retorted. Pesdari rolled her eyes and thought, *"You had just been sleeping a little while ago."*

"Look, what if I sing you that song?"

"The lullaby?"

"Yes."

"Well, only if you sing it the right way," he said. Pesdari frowned.

"My way is the right way."

"No, it's not!" the child protested.

"Yes, it is. Do you want a song or not?"

"...yes."

"Then be quiet."

With that, Pesdari began to sing the lullaby — properly. Among the trees, one of the Dowhas twitched as the words drifted through the night. It drew closer and listened until Pesdari herself fell deep into sleep.

Chapter 13
The Names

Weak sunlight crept through spongy clouds and slid through the cracks in the trio's shelter. Blinking in the tender beams of light, Anicen thought, *"This is the first time I've woken up outside in... I don't even remember how long."*

He relished in the fresh air for a few minutes, almost forgetting about the creeping Dowhas, monstrous rock creatures, and even the torturous time he'd spent underground. Capar shifted in his sleep, and Anicen turned his head to see Pesdari crawling out of the lean-to. Although dark circles painted her eyes, she was feeling revived. She told Anicen she was going to relieve herself and fully emerged into the cool, damp morning. Arms wrapped around herself, she approached a bush that grew just before the trees she was certain hid the Dowhas. Shivering she stared, looking for the ominous shadows. Seeing nothing, she dug a small hole and then squatted down, her eyes constantly shifting to and fro.

"The trees are as black as they are," she thought. She imagined for a moment what it would be like if these frightful shadow creatures had haunted the caves of her former home, where no sunlight at all could have reached them. The hairs on her arms rose at the very idea. Shaking the terrifying image of Dowhas swallowing her in the darkness away, she cleaned herself up with a leaf and returned to the boys. Pesdari flinched

as she caught a whiff of Anicen when he stretched. Then she sniffed herself and frowned.

"We're filthy. Come to the stream," she ordered. The boys, still yawning and stretching themselves awake, groggily did as they were told. The quiet day was interrupted with whoops and yips as they dipped their toes into the cold water. Pesdari thrust her hands into the stream, aggressively rubbing off the grime of her misadventures. She noticed that no other sounds aside from the boys' chicanery and the babble of the stream rose into the air. No birds sang and no tibarbs squeaked from the trees. It was deathly quiet. For the first time, Pesdari really absorbed her surroundings. None of the trees had leaves, she realized. The Yard had been resplendent with turning colors, but here it was as if a malignant disease had swept through the entire forest. The trees' naked, black branches extended like claws. Pesdari's jaw clenched. She couldn't wait to be gone from this place she thought as she finished scrubbing her face and arms. A pile of sumptuous, deep purple berries greeted the trio upon their return from washing up.

"Breakfast!" Capar cheered, grabbing a fistful. Anicen snagged his brother's wrist. He sniffed at the berries before nodding to Capar who greedily threw them all into his mouth. A gift from the Dowhas, Pesdari mused wryly. She turned to the trees, now full of undulating shadows. Laughing, Capar began tossing berries into Anicen's mouth. Her jaw tightened again as she made out several pairs of eyes watching her. They seemed... restless. She had to maintain control over them or else who knew what the Dowhas would do.

"How would Thade handle this?" she wondered. Glancing at the empty tibarb skins strewn on the ground, Pesdari realized the Dowhas that had spoken with her yesterday had very similar ears. Peering at the swirling shadows, she thought she could just see it lurking. She pointed.

"Come here," she commanded haughtily in her best Thade impersonation. The tibarb-eared shadow hovered silently for a moment and then began to glide forward. In the blink of an eye, it was looming over her. The boys took several steps back, their cheerful antics dampened. The creature was almost more horrible to look at in the gray morning. Its impenetrable expanse swallowed any light that touched it.

"I will call you Tibarb unless you have some other name," Pesdari said.

The figure did not move; it seemed stunned.

"Name…" it sighed questioningly, moving closer.

Pesari's lips pinched.

"Yes, a name."

"No... name…"

"Well, now you have one," she grumbled. "Tibarb, you and the rest will keep bringing us food as we travel out of the forest. The gods wish it."

She didn't know if the gods cared if she ate or not, but it wouldn't hurt Tibarb to think that.

"Tibarb... name…," the shadow whispered.

"Yes. Your name is Tibarb."

Anicen growled softly in the direction of the trees.

"Pesdari... they're moving!" Capar yelped. A second Dowhas was moving towards them too swiftly for Pesdari's liking. She gritted her teeth, preparing to release as much fire as she possibly could if need be, but then the Dowhas stopped its approach. Tibarb looked at it. The newcomer was not as tall as Tibarb. It looked more like a block of night with a squat head. As Pesdari watched it warily, it almost seemed to puff out its chest.

"Do those things even have chests?" Anicen wondered. *"Do they have to breathe?"*

"Name," the second Dowhas demanded. Pesdari blinked in surprise.

"You want a name?" she asked it. She looked it over frantically. It didn't have any discerning features as far as she could tell. What would this thing do if she gave it a name it didn't like?

"Um, well-"

"-Star!" Capar called out. The Dowhas looked at him and asked, "Night?"

"Yes! Yer name is Star!" Capar replied confidently as he munched on another berry. Star the Dowhas nodded at him and moved back to the trees whispering, "Name... Star... Star!"

Tibarb didn't leave, but instead made Pesdari very uncomfortable by moving beside her as more Dowhas left the tree cover and drew near.

"Name? Name…" they all began to entreat.

"*They all want names?*" Pesdari wondered as her imagination continued to wither. She stammered trying to think of something to call the shadows. Capar cautiously stepped a little closer to inspect the group. He was starting to grin.

"Your name is Round Eyes. And you're called Nightmare. Mm, you're... you're Shade!"

The Dowhas seemed to approve of their new titles, and the unnamed Dowhas rustled with jealously. More and more came to the little boy to be named. Capar took up the task quite happily.

"Scythe!" he named one shadow creature whose arms curled into deadly points.

"Fang," he solemnly christened another. Anicen, finally in the spirit of things, pointed to a Dowhas who had wings and proclaimed, "Ark! Ark!"

The newly named being flapped its wings with pleasure, at least, Anicen thought it was with pleasure. Its wings expanded wide and with a voice like the wind it declared, "Name... Ark-ark! Ark-ark!"

Ark-ark's name was repeated several times by the group as another slithered its way forward. Capar rubbed his chin studiously as he inspected the unnamed shadow. It was tall and skinny with tendrils that swirled in the air.

"Your name is Tree," he declared. Tree was delighted, but

Anicen looked at his brother with befuddlement. Capar shrugged.

"I like trees!" he said. All the while, Pesdari stood still as stone next to Tibarb. She was uncomfortable with the silent guard. Why was it standing next to her? She wanted Tibarb to go away, but she sank her nails into her palms to keep herself calm. After the naming ceremony had come to a close, Pesdari took a step away from her unwanted guard.

"It's time to go," she declared. She turned on her heel and began to walk, following the stream. The newly named conclave of shadows escorted the trio, an almost playful air to their movements now. Much to her chagrin, Pesdari realized that Tibarb followed closely at her heel. She began to speak to hide her unease.

"Another comes from the Coven. Her name is Thade, and she must die," Pesdari said.

"Coven?" Tibarb whispered.

"It doesn't matter that she's from the Coven!" Pesdari snapped. "She must die! The gods command it."

An echo of a much younger Thade laughed in her head. Looking ahead, Pesdari saw two little girls making crowns of brilliant green leaves. With a grimace, the vision was gone. She strode on in silence.

Chapter 14

The Father

Capar was chattering at the Dowhas as they carried forth, but as the tepid light began to dissolve even he became quiet. It was early evening when a voice broke the still air. Pesdari quickly moved behind a tree. Anicen and Capar mimicked her. A man was crouching down by the stream, humming to himself.

"What is he doing here? Doesn't he know this place is dangerous?" Anicen thought. Pesdari couldn't get a very good look at the man, because suddenly Nightmare and Sycthe were flying at him — two streaks of murderous night. The man had but a moment to scream before he was engulfed by the shadows. Pesdari's lips parted but she made no sound. The boys stared in horror. All three were stunned into silence by the speed of the attack. Then, Sycthe and Nightmare drifted away from the man's lifeless body. Slowly, what Anicen thought was black smoke slithered out of the man's mouth and nose.

It rose into the air, twisting and pulling at itself. At last, a shape began to emerge from the mass. Two long horns grew out of what Pesdari assumed was a head. Then two milky white eyes seemed to be carved out of the shadow. The newly created Dowhas stared at the group of humans and its brethren. It slowly began to move towards them. Pesdari clenched her jaw as it approached. Tibarb looked at her.

"Safe…"

Pesdari glanced at Tibarb suspiciously. She had just watched two of the Dowhas kill a man that she wouldn't have called a threat by any stretch of the imagination. Tibarb gestured to the body.

"Rest... Eat…"

Anicen emitted a disgusted whine at the suggestion. Capar went pale, clutching at his ragged shirt nervously. Pesdari snorted in distaste before saying, "No. We will not rest here by a corpse, and we will *not* eat it. We will camp further on. Go find us food."

Her voice was more calm than her stomach. Tibarb didn't move at first. Pesdari's stomach clenched. Could these things actually take offense? Then, without a word, Tibarb glided away into the forest.

Ark-Ark took the lead and led the group past the dead man. The boys stared at their feet as they passed. Anicen made sure they walked far enough away so that not even a speck of the unfortunate victim was visible to them. When they stopped to make camp, Tibarb appeared. The voluminous shadow dropped three more tibarbs at Pesdari's feet. Pesdari refused to make a fire that night. A large blister had formed on her finger from the night before.

Anicen growled at her.

"I don't want to," she snarled back. "You do it."

With an aggravated huff, Anicen took his stone knife and approached the trees. He took a large branch from the ground and began to break off its minor shoots. Capar joined him as he carved at the branch until a section of it was smooth.

"I remember Pa doing this!" Capar exclaimed. "Don't yah need another stick?"

Anicen nodded, and his little brother loped off to find one. It took the young boy a few tries to find one his brother approved of, but at last, he succeeded. Ancien took the shorter piece of wood and worked at it with his knife until it came to a rounded point. Sitting on the large branch he started to aggressively rub the smaller stick along it. Pesdari watched the show with a grumbling stomach but it was too late to give in now. She marveled at how long it was taking for Anicen to produce fire.

"How do any of you eat?" she jeered. Anicen ignored her. Back and forth the stick moved until delicate tendrils of smoke began to rise. Quickly, he moved the small coal he had created into a pile of kindling. After a few minutes of tender care, their fire crackled and snapped in the night. The trio ate their meal in silence.

The boys fell asleep quickly. As they breathed in the night air, Tibarb approached Pesdari.

"Name…" whispered Tibarb. Pesdari glowered at the shadow's haunting eyes.

"Your name is Tibarb. Have you really forgotten already?" she asked.

"No... name," Tibarb said again, this time gesturing to Pesdari.

She furrowed her brow.

"My name?" she asked. Tibarb nodded.

"My name is Pesdari," she said cautiously.

"A... child's name. M-my child's... name," the shadow breathed. Pesdari thought she heard mourning in its voice.

"You have a child?" she asked, stunned.

"Had... have..."

"I don't understand."

Tibarb suddenly stopped moving and before Pesdari could even gasp, she was engulfed by shadow. She blinked and saw a rushing river. A woman, no, Rothme. Her name was Rothme. She had dark brown hair in two braids and was skinning tibarbs as she smiled at a little laughing girl.

"Pesdari!" boomed a deep, cheerful voice. Pesdari balked when the little girl turned and looked at her.

"Poppa!"

The little girl ran to him — no, Pesdari realized. The little girl was running to *her*. Somehow she was watching these events through another person's eyes. That woman looked so much like someone she had known before. The man tossed the girl into the air, and the light shifted.

"Pesdari, you must sleep now."

"No, Poppa, I am not tired," pouted little Pesdari.

"Should I sing to you?"

"Yes!"

The lullaby that came made Pesdari's blood run cold. She knew those words. She knew that voice.

"What is this!" she tried to scream, but the man's voice kept singing the soothing words until Pesdari watched the child fall asleep.

The scene was different again. She was hunting. It had been a prosperous day. Six tibarb were already slung behind her, no, *his* back. It was time to go home. Then pounding hooves, snorting in the air. Mounted riders appeared almost out of nowhere, emitting wild cries. They were everywhere!

Vuglar. The word pounded in Pesdari's head.

Vuglar.

And then, pain. Sharp, horrible pain ricocheted throughout Pesdari as the mounted riders cheered.

Pesdari — no, she reminded herself — *the man* crawled through the grass towards black trees, desperate for escape.

The Vuglar will not come into the trees.

Breathing was agony. Moving torture. Once inside the cool embrace of the forest, all the man wanted to do was lie still. A rest, just a little rest, and then home. Home to Rothme... Pesdari. A shadow filled Pesdari's vision, a shadow that looked like Ark-Ark. Horrible wings were swept out wide for just a moment before it descended.

Pesdari blinked again, and she was a shadow. She felt nothing but a mild chill. She moved through trees of night. She killed a woman lost in the forest and greedily devoured the warmth of her. There was no joy in the killings. No true satisfaction. Simply an instinct to kill all who entered Yrecep Forest, to feel warmth again for just a moment. Then she waited for the new dark thing that would arise from the corpse. She led the newly arisen shadow to the others. None spoke. What seemed like hundreds of milky white eyes watched her.

The spell was broken.

Strands of inky blackness pulled away from Pesdari's skin like brambles. Her heart was racing and her eyes were frantic with heartache as she stared at Tibarb.

"Are you alive?" she demanded to know.

"No... no..." he replied with dreadful pauses between his words. Shock and sorrow rendered Pesdari speechless.

"Pesdari, Pesdari. My child... my child..."

The shadow wrapped around her shoulders in a mockery of an embrace. Pesdari's face was enveloped in the cold expanse of her father's transfigured form as, at last, she began to sob.

In the morning, Capar and Anicen awoke to find Pesdari staring listlessly at the stream. Looking over her shoulder, she said, "It's time to go."

Her voice was unusually quiet. The boys exchanged a glance. Something was clearly wrong, but they did as they were told. As they walked, the Dowhas followed until Anicen barked happily. The stream had led them to a river, a river that followed away from the realm of the murky, unwelcoming forest.

"Is that... is that a river?" Pesdari asked, squinting at the rushing body of water.

"Of course it is!" Capar replied.

"It's strange to see it in the light. I've only ever seen its shadow."

"Come on! Let's go!" cheered Capar, not paying attention to anything but the way ahead. He could see a bridge in the distance, and a group of children running down a hill.

Pesdari took one last look at the forms of the Dowhas

blinking away like an afterthought. Only the tall eared shadow wavered at the edge of the trees, looking as if it was trying to follow her.

Chapter 15

The Witch

Cigma the Witch, as the town children had dubbed her, was still wrapped in her nightclothes and nibbling on her breakfast of scrambled egg and bread slathered with honey when a ruddy-cheeked girl popped her head through the door.

"Good morning, Cigma!" crowed the little girl.

"It could have been, Yslil," the old woman replied dryly. Yslil's grin spread from ear to ear as giggles erupted from behind the door. Before Cigma knew it, children were practically bouncing off the ceiling demanding all sorts of nonsense. As she doggedly chewed her bread, a currant-haired boy stuck his happy freckled face much too close to hers.

"Turn Sociun into a bug, Cigma! She tattled on me!" he demanded, pointing at another girl whose hair matched his own.

"You deserved it, Coripeus!" retorted Sociun, her face slightly pale at the prospect of becoming a creepy, crawling thing.

Cigma kept chewing as she stared expectantly for the rest of the story. He tilted his head sheepishly and smirked.

"Well, I *did* take a sausage from Butcher Reb without asking."

Cigma's free hand lashed out and flicked Coripeus's upturned nose. He clutched it as Sociun howled with laughter.

Cigma poked the admitted thief's forehead.

"That was for stealing. We don't steal from our friends. That's a nasty thing to do, Cori."

Before the chastisement sunk too deep, she produced a little green stone from her pocket.

"And this is for telling the truth," she said before tossing a blue one to Sociun.

"Soci, this is for keeping your cousin honest."

All past sins forgotten, the cousins set about comparing their treasures.

"I wuv you, Cigma!" exclaimed a little voice from the folds of the woman's skirts. Cigma stole a glance away from the pandemonium threatening to destroy her home. She could only see his tightly braided rows of hair, but she knew who the child was immediately. She snatched the little one up, her head whipping around the room irritably.

"Torbeh! Come get your baby brother this instant! You know your momma doesn't like little Gilbins wandering off. Why are all you rascals here anyway?"

A handsome boy with braids longer and more resplendent braids bounded over.

"The festival! Today's the start of the festival!" he said, holding out his arms for his baby brother, but the little one wanted nothing to do with him and snuggled closer to Cigma.

"I may be old, Torbeh, but I've not lost my mind. I know very well that the festival is this time of year, *every* year."

"You are *very* old," an unseen rascal chimed in.

"We keep expecting you to be dead, but you never are!" Yslil remarked cheerfully.

"Gili, you must let go now, dear," Cigma said as she aimed a pointed look at Yslil, who hid in mock terror behind Cori. The old woman detached Gilbins from around her neck and handed him to Torbeh. Glaring at all the children now, her gnarled forefingers danced along her thumbs.

"I'm not dead, but *you* all might be if you don't let me

enjoy my breakfast in peace!" she threatened. Glittering flashes of light leaped from her hands. The children screamed with ecstatic terror.

"She's sparking mad now!"

"Run!"

Before Cori scampered off with his mates, he turned and called back, "There's a mage this year, Cigma! You have to come!"

"Shoo! Begone, you little miscreants! I'll come, I'll come just give me some peace!" she called out, flapping her hands at the delighted group. She leaned against the doorway and chuckled.

"Silly little beasts," she thought, watching the children scamper down the dirt path from her door towards a stone bridge that crossed a narrow section of the Hringus River. The bridge brought travelers to the other section of the path which ran straight towards the town's walls. If Cigma were to turn to the right, her sight would rest on the edge of Yrecep Forest. She always tried very hard not to look in that direction. She kept her eyes firmly on the gaggle of children to be sure they all were heading towards the safety of the town. In the distance, she could hear braying beasts of burden and other shouts that marked the festival. A crisp breeze filled her lungs and turned her cheeks pink.

"What a lovely morning," Cigma smiled, till something interrupted her mind's pleasant embrace of the day. A voice, distant yet familiar, pulled at her thoughts. Cigma frowned, wondering if one of the children was playing a trick on her. Wind suddenly began to buffet her. The old woman's frowning turned to a strangled cry as the voice of Egal seared her mind.

"Loooook toooo thhhhe forrrreeeesssst."

Shocked, Cigma grasped the door frame. Her eyes turned away from the path and to the accursed place. She couldn't believe what she was seeing. Children were running from the black trees. Of all the things Cigma knew, this was an undeniable truth: No ordinary person left Yrecep Forest.

Behind the two smaller figures slowly walked what appeared to be a young woman.

"Has the Coven finally come for me after all this time?" Cigma thought frantically. She turned to hide within her home, but the wind howled upon her. The sudden gale didn't stop until she once again faced the approaching figures. Before she knew it, there they were on her doorstep. The young woman wiped at her eyes. Cigma squinted — were those tears?

"Hello, grandmother!" a little boy greeted her warmly. Cigma placed a hand on her chest. Calling older women 'grandmother' was a custom of the plains folk. What was this child doing so far from his home and coming from the forest no less?

"Child, what-" but Cigma couldn't finish her own question. Horns were curling from the boy's heads. She snapped her neck around to look closer at the three strangers. An older boy was trying to hide his face, but Cigma's eyes were sharp. She recoiled at the sight of his muzzle.

Pesdari watched the old woman stagger back into an unfamiliar structure. It was a creation unlike any she had ever seen. It didn't seem to be a part of the earth at all but rather sat on top of the dirt and grass.

"In the gods' names... what has been done to you!" the old woman exclaimed.

"Can we rest here?" Pesdari injected coldly, putting her hands upon the boys' shoulders, getting ready to throw them to the side in case she needed to fight. The old woman gaped like a fish before nodding and ushering them in. Pesdari eyed the wooden posts that rose up before her suspiciously and hesitated, but the boys walked right inside without fear. The old woman, whose composure was returning, watched her.

"Listen. My name is Cigma. You're safe here. Did you come... did you come from the Coven?" she asked, her voice wavering. Pesdari glared at her coldly. The boys froze. Anicen gripped his brother's shoulder, ready to run.

"What do you know of the Coven?"

Cigma snorted, growing more assured by the second.

"Calm yourself. I was of the Coven once too."

"You lie."

"As it is in nature, as it is with the gods, let it be so with you," Cigma said, her voice bitter. She spat on the floor as soon as the prayer left her lips. Anicen and Capar watched the exchange in quiet fascination.

"You escaped," Pesdari said. Cigma nodded. After a moment, Pesdari took a tentative step forward, peeking over her head as if she expected the whole thing to collapse on her. Once she was inside, she was rooted to the spot. Out of the corner of her eye, she could see a beautiful woman sitting next to a man. She blinked and had the strangest sensation that she had been in this place before. The muscles in her eye twitched. No, she had never been here before, but once, long ago, she had lived somewhere very much like this. She had lived there with a mother and a father. Once upon a time, she remembered mournfully, she had been part of a loving family. She thought of her father locked forever in Yrecep Forest's embrace and dug her nails into her palm to keep calm. She looked to Cigma.

"A person could escape the caves alone, but how did you get out of the forest?"

Cigma raised her hands. The skin from her fingers to her elbows was stretched in patchy colors, a marbling of scar tissue.

"The only way was by becoming a living sacrifice to Riefon," she told Pesdari. She rubbed her knuckles as the unpleasant memory rose in her mind.

"A shadow can't swallow a living torch. I seemed to spend an eternity in that forest."

Pesdari could see it now. Those arms bearing fire for however long Cigma had been lost. No one in the Coven was powerful enough to sustain flames like that and remain unscathed — except for Thade, Pesdari thought wryly. She cast her eyes over the old woman's mangled hands. The pain must have been excruciating.

Moving around her home, Cigma said, "You will all stay here for now. It has been many years since I've talked with one of my brethren. Is Divorc still alive?"

Pesdari nodded.

"What a pity. Ah, well. Boys, have you been fed? You look half starved," she remarked, handing them two thick pieces of bread.

"Thank yah, grandmother!" Capar piped up. Anicen gave a little yip. He immediately regretted it as Cigma eyed him, but all the old woman said was, "You're far from home, aren't you? What are your names?"

"I'm Capar, and that's my brother Anicen. He can't talk."

Tap. Tap. Tap. Tap-tap.

"I'm not an idiot! It's true! Yah can't talk!"

Cigma chuckled with approval.

"Clever thing, aren't you? You poor boy. Well, at least whatever happened to you left you human in your mind. Sit, you two. Sit, and tell me your story," she said, retrieving a needle, thread, and some fabric from a corner of the room.

This was an instruction Capar didn't need to hear twice. He immediately launched into the tale. Anicen tried desperately to intervene when his brother got off kilter, but he needn't have bothered. Cigma kept the child in line as he recounted how his village was about to be raided by Vuglar. and to save them, their parents had told them to hide in Yrecep Forest where a mysterious woman tricked them into drinking water that put them in a deep sleep. When they awoke underground, they were Thade's prisoners and subjected to horrible experiments. Brows knit close, Cigma interrupted Capar. Her face was hard as she looked at Pesdari.

"Who is this Thade?" she asked.

"A monster," Pesdari said calmly, ignoring the memory of

two young girls magically blowing fallen leaves into colorful tornadoes that played behind her eyes.

"And then Pesdari found us! She helped us escape!" Capar told the old woman. Cigma nodded slowly, using her teeth to sever the last bit of thread.

"That... that is quite the tale, little one. Here. See if this fits on your head."

She held up a rather ramshackle yet durable hood for the boy. Without question, Capar pulled it on. It was a bit baggy, but the old woman nodded with satisfaction.

"That will hide your horns from any Nosy Netties," she told him.

"Thank yah, grandmother!"

Cigma nodded at Anicen.

"And you will get something soon enough to hide your face. A scarf maybe. It will be cold soon. No one will think twice about you covering up."

Sharp knocking on the cottage door brought a tense quiet to the room. Motioning for her guests to be still, Cigma opened the door just a crack. A man in dazzling robes with a sable-colored staff in his hand stood outside. Four other large fellows waited behind him, none of them looking altogether friendly. Cigma pursed her lips.

"What do you want?"

"My good lady, I am the mage Garanort! I have been advised that you have some of the finest magical ingredients stored in your, ah, *lovely* home," the mage said, eyeing Cigma's cottage with unbridled distaste.

"Yes, yes, I'm sure I have something for you. What do you need?"

Inside, Pesdari almost laughed. A real mage in the flesh! She'd have to tell Thade. Pesdari shook her head. That friendship was demolished, she reminded herself.

"You were going to kill her, remember? And now she's coming to kill you."

She couldn't hear what the mage asked for but as Cigma turned to retrieve the requested item, the old woman tripped on a discarded scrap of fabric. Anicen had been taking care not to face the door, but on instinct, he rushed to help her. The door creaked open. Pesdari could now see the mage's face. Anicen whipped his head away, and Pesdari couldn't tell if the mage's light eyebrows were raised in shock at the boy's muzzle or if he simply was concerned for the old woman's well-being.

Flustered, Cigma quickly grabbed a small bundle of herbs hanging from her ceiling and gave them to the mage.

"Ah, my dear lady, you have company. I won't bother you further. Thank you very much!" Garanort said as he handed a gold piece to Cigma.

"This is too much."

"Not at all! After all, I've disturbed your little gathering. Be well, and have a happy Festival!"

Then the mage turned on his heel and his not-so-merry band went after him.

Chapter 16
The Kidnapping

Bugs and frogs sang together in a nocturnal chorus outside the cottage. Inside, logs were popping and snapping in the fire. Anicen and Capar, curled up like two pups on some blankets before Cigma's humble mantle, happily drowsed off. Although she too was tired and pleasantly warmed by the thick robe Cigma had given her, a thin line of suspicion kept Pesdari alert as she sat at the table with the old witch. Cigma seemingly paid her no mind at all as she poured a currant-colored liquid into two cups. Pesdari stared at the cup offered to her.

"It's not poison," Cigma scoffed. "You're not in the Coven anymore. I'd say you only need to worry about being killed half the day now."

Cigma's rolled her eyes at Pesdari's stony expression. Exasperated, she took a sip from both cups.

"It's mulled wine. See? *Try* it," she pressed.

Pesdari frowned but did cautiously taste the foreign concoction. Her perplexed tongue buzzed. She licked her lips, unsure of how she felt about the beverage. On the other hand, her feelings toward the old witch were slowly growing warmer.

"What will you do with them?" Cigma asked her. Pesdari looked up with slightly less wariness and shrugged.

"Bring them to their home, I suppose. I have nothing else to do," she replied absently, still dazzled by the flavors on her tongue. She took another sip as Cigma scowled at her before glancing at Anicen and Capar. Both were now deep into their slumber.

"Even if their parents survived that raid, you think their people will accept those boys now? They're cursed creatures! They'll be lucky if they last a day!" Cigma hissed. "You must fix whatever... whatever that Thade did to them."Pesdari glared back, gesturing wildly at the sleeping boys.

"How?" she snarled in a whisper. "How do I fix *that*?"

The other woman leaned back and rubbed her wrinkled face. She gazed at the unlucky brothers. Their serene sleeping faces asleep before the crackling logs would have made for a beautiful scene if they weren't so awfully afflicted, she thought.

"Pray to those damnable gods of ours," Cigma finally said, her voice leaden. Pesdari snorted and raised the wine to her lips. She rebelliously let all of the contents slide down her gullet.

"As if they would care about fixing them. They'd sooner have them wiped clean from the circle," she thought bitterly. Cigma folded her arms, watching the young woman.

"Why have you taken them?" she asked. Pesdari lowered her cup, her expression surly.

"What does it matter?"

Cigma raised her eyebrows at Pesdari's aggressive tone.

"I'm just curious."

Shifting her eyes to the floor, Pesdari watched the firelight flicker off of Capar's horns. Her thoughts felt as if they were blanketed in heavy snow, but images of Capar launching himself at Thade to knock her down, and Anicen's gnashing jaws on her former friend's arm drifted through like snowflakes.

"They saved me from death," she replied. "It felt... right to give them a chance."

Cigma tilted her head in mild surprise.

"Strange for you to think that way. The Coven certainly didn't teach you that. Die and let die was how things were when I was there."

"Things still are that way," Pesdari replied. "That's why I left. I wanted to live." She jerked her chin towards the boys. "They wanted to live too. We were useful to each other."

Cigma nodded slowly.

"I understand. You are free now though. Why keep them with you?"

Pesdari looked anywhere but at the old woman as her cheeks flushed.

"I told you. It feels right."

A little smile playing at her lips, Cigma stood.

"So, she is growing a conscience. I wonder how she'll like it," she thought. Then aloud she said, "Be warned — tell no one where you came from. Our kind is feared, rumored about, and there are those who seek to exploit our skills. Fear and greed are both powerful motivators to do harm."

Pesdari listened, fingers playing with the cup. With a yawn, Cigma continued.

"That's enough talk for tonight. I have another blanket. I'll fetch it fo-"

An explosion rocked the cottage. Wood and dirt careened through the space. Flying through the air, Pesdari slammed against a far wall. Her ears rang so terribly, she could barely hear the shouts of the men who rushed into the room. Cigma was shouting too, trying to get to her feet. Anicen, now fully awake, began tossing debris off himself and his brother. Pesdari blinked slowly. Nothing sounded quite right. She was a slug and quick birds were flitting all around her.

"Garanort, you beast!" Cigma yelled. The mage haughtily stood in the cottage's ragged new opening, his staff raised in his hand.

"That's the one! Grab him!" boomed Garanort from the cottage's orifice, pointing straight at Anicen. Grabbing their target by the hair and shoulders, two of Garanort's thugs shoved a sack over the boy's head. A third hit Capar in the face as he tried to help his brother. The young child sprawled on his back, stunned.

"My apologies, my good lady, but I couldn't let such a marvel remain in the hands of a country bumpkin!" Garanort laughed. "He's invaluable! A true magical find!"

"Leave him alone!" Cigma shouted, flicking her fingers together. Sparks began to fly. Garanort sneered at the woman as he aimed his staff at her, muttering something. Jagged bits of debris assailed Cigma. She fell back, clutching at her side. Through hazy eyes, Pesdari watched Anicen kick and lash around until one of the men slammed a piece of wood down on his head. Just as the boy slumped, she blinked into nothing.

...

"Wake up! Wake up! They took Anicen!"

Acquiescing the request was painful. She didn't want to do it, but Pesdari did open her eyes if only to squint at Capar. Boiling over with anxiety, the little boy was shaking her shoulders hard. Nausea rolled through her with every movement. "Stop," groaned Pesdari. Her head was pounding. Shakily rising to her feet, she began to survey the damage. Cigma was sitting on the floor, hands covered in blood. The old woman looked up, a nightshirt pressed hard against her side. Capar's head swiveled between the two women, unsure of what to do. Panic was writ large across his face.

"You're wounded," Pesdari noted stupidly. Cigma snorted at the obvious statement then winced.

"The cut's not too deep. I still remember a few old healing tricks. I'll be fine," she wheezed. "They took one of your charges," she continued through gritted teeth. Pesdari wobbled towards her.

"Do you... do you have, um, a poultice?" she asked. Words

rose sluggishly to her mind, unwieldy and elusive.

"What is wrong with me?" she thought, rubbing at her temples.

"Leave me!" Cigma ordered. She pointed to the door. "Go after them!"

With that, Capar was running out of the ruined cottage after his brother, clutching at his hood. Pesdari tried to keep up with the young boy, but every step split her head with pain. They raced down the path and over the bridge, the sounds of people and commerce growing louder. As the defensive stone wall of the town loomed over them, Capar paused in awe.

"The big town," he breathed. Pesdari was grateful for the momentary rest. Her stomach was threatening to unload its contents any second now. Night air calmed her as she sucked it down her lungs, but then they were running again, straight through the gates.

Despite the late hour, the town was dancing with light. Sounds bombarded Pesdari. Gray animals she had never seen before with pointed ears brayed irritably as their stocky legs stomped against a stone-lined street. Strange creatures walked high overhead in checkered clothes, and her face went pale at the sight of their clattering wooden feet. Vomit surged in Pesdari's throat. She pressed herself against a wall, relieving her body of its burdens. Passersby barked with laughter.

"Festival's just started!" a shrill woman jeered.

"Gone and had too much already, eh?" someone else taunted her. Disoriented and afraid, Pesdari wheeled through a doorway. She collided hard with a man who grabbed her arms.

"Hey! What are you running from, girl?"

"Get off me!"

"Hold on, hold on! You ran into me, remember?"

"No — what? I... oh," muttered Pesdari, sinking to the floor.

"Pesdari!" Capar cried from the doorway.

"What's wrong with her, boy?" the bewildered man asked

as the child rushed to Pesdari's side.

"These young folk get wilder every year. I tell you, this foolishness is enough to drive me to Yrecep Forest!" the man huffed.

"Get up, Pesdari, please, please, please get up!" begged Capar

"W-water," Pesdari mumbled to him. With tears in his eyes, Capar looked at the man.

"Please! Give her water!"

The still surprised man tugged at his long blonde beard in disbelief but fetched a small waterskin. He handed it to Capar who immediately held it to Pesdari's lips. She drank deep, the taste of vomit corroding her tongue.

"Is she sick?" the man asked, clearly worried that whatever this stranger had was catching.

"No…" Pesdari groaned. "I hit my head."

The man chewed on his lip, deliberating, before he said, "Look, you're in no shape to go running around. Rest here for a moment."

"We can't! My brother-" Capar began.

"-The mage Garanort stole something from us," Pesdari managed to say through clenched teeth. Her head was a drum again. The man immediately raised his hands and stepped back.

"Whatever grief you have with this Garanort, I don't want to hear it. You're rattled something awful though. I've got a small pen in the back that's warm and clean. You're welcome to sleep there."

Too discombobulated to do anything but accept the man's request, Pesdari used Capar to pull herself upright.

"Yes."

"Alright," Capar mumbled, discouraged that they couldn't continue the search for Anicen. Somewhere in the murky depths of her mind, Pesdari remembered the phrase Capar had used to express gratitude.

"Th-thank you," she stammered, unsure if she got it right.

The man nodded curtly.

"I'm Borblec. Bo for short. Follow me."

He promptly strode out the front door and turned left. A narrow alley led to, as promised, a small pen with a trough before it. One of those gray animals that Pesdari had seen earlier was standing in front of the pen, chewing on its dinner.

"You've got company, Shaggy," said Bo. "Be polite."

"Here, Pesdari, lie down in the hay," Capar said. Despite his worry for Anicen, he was eager to pet the donkey. He felt like he hadn't seen one for an eternity. Shaggy, the donkey, was a gentle creature. He let the boy scratch him behind the ears and wasn't all too bothered by the strange visitor crushing his hay. He saw his master watching the newcomers. His master said something. Shaggy didn't recognize any of those words as his commands, so he continued chewing and enjoying his scratches.

"You can rest here, but you'll need to be gone by first light."

Pesdari nodded. The thought of moving made her queasy. As Bo left them, Capar sat down next to Pesdari. His worry chewed at him.

"What'll we do?" he asked her in a small voice. She cast him a sidelong glance, feeling ill.

"Sleep. Then we'll look for Anicen," she murmured already closing her eyes. Shaggy seemingly heard the suggestion too and moved closer. He folded himself down to rest. The little boy, whose face was wet with tears snuggled up to him, and all three were soon fast asleep.

Chapter 17

The Rescue

Pesdari and Capar rose with the dawn. After giving Shaggy a few more scratches on his chin, Capar called out to his guardian as she began to walk away.

"Aren't we going to leave anything for Bo?"

"Why?"

"He let us sleep here!"

"He never asked for anything."

"But it's good manners!"

Pesdari paused, she was feeling much better and wanted to be on her way. Sighing, she kept her irritation in check.

"What would he want? We have nothing to give him," she replied. The boy tugged at an imaginary beard, then pointed at Shaggy's trough.

"We could fill the trough? It's almost empty."

Pesdari peered at the trough that was, as Capar noticed, nearly depleted of water. Pesdari didn't quite understand what the trough was for, but if water had to go into it, she supposed she could help. The air was damp, and dew glistened all around the small yard. She stood there with her arms by her side, elbows slightly bent so her fingers pointed out. Her hands looked expectant as if waiting for someone to hold them. Fingers curling gently, Pesdari reached out to the dew around her. Individual droplets began to gravitate towards the trough.

The droplets melded with each other until one large ball of water was slowly rolling over the lip of the trough. As soon as it finished its climb, the water broke free and sloshed into its resting place. Capar nodded happily. The trough was now half full.

"That should do it!"

"I'm so glad you're pleased," Pesdari drawled, turning on her heel. Securing his hood around his head, Capar followed her. Making their way down the alley, they bumped into Bo who was carrying a basket full of bread and meat. He appeared quite relieved that they were leaving as instructed. Perhaps that's why he bothered telling them, "That mage you mentioned, missy, he's getting all set to leave."

"What? How do you know?" Capar exclaimed.

"Not many mages around these parts. He sticks out like a sore thumb. I happened to see him on my way to the baker. They're tearing down his festival stall right now."

"Where is he!" Pesdari snapped. Quickly, Bo stammered out the directions. Capar was off like a bird on the wind, and Pesdari soon overtook him. Running set her head to aching a little again, but her senses had returned to her. She felt refreshed — and vengeful.

The town with its crowded structures still overwhelmed her a bit. Many times she and Capar would stare at intersecting roads, painfully deliberating whether to turn left or right. Yet, by some miracle, they properly followed Bo's directions. Pesdari had just turned a corner when she caught sight of Garanort ordering his men about. She and Capar ducked behind an unattended stall. The street was empty still but for Garanort and his crew. Capar peaked over Pesdari's shoulder for a better look. It was just as Bo had said, the mage was getting ready to make a hasty exit.

"Quickly now!" Garanort ordered his men as he leaned against a wagon, staff in hand. He was flamboyantly dressed. An amethyst turban sat upon his head and a crimson scarf was draped about his shoulders. Anicen stood next to him, a sack still over his head and his hands bound. A rope secured him to the back of the wagon. Indignation and fear surged in Capar's chest at the treatment of his brother. Without warning, he emerged from his hiding place and shouted, "Give me back my brother!"

"You idiot!" Pesdari snarled under her breath before stepping out to join the child. Garanort looked surprised for a moment, but then he laughed. "No! Whatever has happened to your brother needs to be studied. That old witch certainly doesn't have the education to do it. Your brother is *much* better off in my hands!"

"*You stupid, arrogant idiot*," Pesdari seethed. Images of gales and screaming winds swept through her mind. She lifted her arms high overhead and whipped her hands forward as if she were throwing something heavy at the mage. Garanot and his men nearly lost their footing as a fierce wind buffeted him. Anicen clutched to the wagon as the wind careened down the street. Furious, Garanort pointed his staff at Pesdari and began to whisper. Capar ducked as a fist-sized fireball hurtled at Pesdari. She whipped her head to the right, but her streaming hair was singed off as it passed by followed by a crash in the distance and screaming as some poor towns person found their house on fire.

A bald guard dashed over and swung at Pesdari with a long knife, cutting a wicked path across the front of her thigh. She screamed, staggered back, and then slammed her hands on the ground. All the rocks and pebbles around her flew at the bald man. He grunted as the bombardment collided with his face, the force of Pesdari's will pushing the little stones through his skull. His lifeless body fell back, and Pesdari pressed forward toward Garanort. He raised the strange staff again, still muttering. Anicen kicked out blindly and managed to strike the mage's back interrupting whatever spell Garanort had been about to cast. Snarling, the mage struck Anicen across the head and shoulders with his staff.

Another guard was between Pesdari and the mage. He was slight but fast. Pesdari tried to remove him with a second barrage of stones, but he was too quick and avoided the attack. The wagon rattled with the impact of the small missiles. Crouching, the man rushed Pesdari. Just a step or two away, he raised a cudgel to strike her down. Instead of running, Pesdari stood her ground. She lunged at him, grabbed his face in her hands, and pulled it close to hers. She began to forcefully inhale. Eyes bulging and face turning purple with consternation, the man tried to shake her off, but Pesdari's nails had sunk deep into his cheeks. She would not let go. All the air in his lungs raced out to Pesdari's beckoning lips. Garanort gaped as his guard began to go limp in Pesdari's grasp. The two remaining thugs stared at their master in confused terror.

"What are you!" the mage yelled at Pesdari. "Some sort of sorceress?"

She didn't bother answering. Pain and rage pushed her forward. Blood ran down her leg as she limped closer to the men. One turned and ran. Fuming at this betrayal, Garanort quickly whispered to his staff and slammed it down.

"AARGH!" cried his remaining guard as the street began to rumble below. Pesdari fell to the ground, but in the corner of her eye, she saw Capar creeping closer and closer to the mage. Garanort clung to his staff laughing manically as stalls fell apart at the force of the quaking spasms. Finally, the trembling came to an end. Garanort panted heavily and kicked out at his final, trembling, guard.

"Get. Up," he hissed at the cowering man. Then he turned his scornful gaze at Pesdari.

"Quit while you can. You have some skill, but you are no match for me!"

Seizing his chance, Capar ran forward. His curled horns smashed into the mage's back.

"Unf!"

The mage's grip gave way, and his staff sailed in Pesdari's direction, clattering before her. She grabbed it, and with terror in his eyes, the final guard raced after his compatriot. Garanort stared, horrified, as Pesdari used his own staff to stand. Seeing red, Pesdari quickly closed the distance between them. Garanort leaped to his feet, but he was too late. The staff swung at him, connecting with his chin, and sending him sprawling onto his back. Pesdari's shadow stretched over him. The pointed tip of the staff raised high in the air.

"No, wait! Stop!" Garanort begged. He raised his hands, defenseless, but he could see no mercy rested in the young woman. Her mind wiped clean with fury, Pesdari slammed the staff's tip into Garanort's chest. Eyes wide, he coughed up a wave of blood with a hideous gurgle. The whole thing was shockingly quiet, despite the ferocity of Pesdari's pounding blood. The street's emptiness magnified the terrible squelching that accompanied Pesdari's attempts to pull the staff out of Garanort's chest. Capar gaped at the dead mage but quickly turned to free his brother.

Pesdari grabbed her bloody thigh as blood lust subsided and pain moved to the forefront of her mind. She hobbled over to the dead man who had sliced her thigh and took his knife. With it, she cut a long strip of fabric from his shirt and tied it around her wound. She would have to clean it later, she thought to herself and dropped the knife with a clatter.

"Quickly! This way!" hissed a voice from between two stalls. Capar looked up to see a young woman wrapped head to toe in cobalt and bright yellow robes. A small harp hung by a leather strap over her shoulder.

"Quick! Before the guards come!" she ordered again. Anicen ripped the scarf away from the dead Garanort and tied it around his face to hide his appearance. Capar rushed to the woman, rapidly followed by Anicen and Pesdari, the staff still in her hand. Muffled shouting could be heard coming their way.

"Follow me," the woman said, running through an alley concealed by the stalls. In silence, the group followed the stranger through twisting back alleys and pressed themselves against walls as town guards ran to the site of the battle. Anicen kept his head low as they made their escape.

"We need to get out of town till this dies down," whispered the woman. "I'll get you through the gates."

The woman led them as promised out of the town as if committing acts of subterfuge were her daily occupation. Once they had cleared the bridge, they left the path to Cigma's cottage and began to move around the hill, walking in the long grass. After checking to be sure no one was around them, the woman whipped around with a wide smile on her dimpled cheeks.

"Are you a mage too?" she asked Pesdari. "How wonderful! I'll show all those idiots at the Cathedral what a true saga is!" she gloated.

"Pesdari! She's a cantor!" Capar cried, ecstatically. He had only seen a cantor at his village once when he was very little, but he remembered the wonderful songs and stories that had filled the day and even much of the night. The cantor swept her cloak out like the wings of an enormous bird and curtsied dramatically.

"Nyfun, Cantor Second-Class, at your service!"

Pesdari grimaced at the showboating, perplexed by this individual.

"I'm not a mage," she said, her voice flat.

"Oh, really? What are you called?" Nyfun asked eagerly. Pesdari narrowed her eyes in suspicion.

"Pesdari."

Nyfun tapped a finger to her lips and considered this.

"No, no that simply won't do," she murmured, still quite cheerful. Pesdari frowned.

"Why not?"

"It's incredibly boring. Here, I'll help you. This is *my* saga after all, so I think it's only right that I help my characters achieve greatness. Professor Gribon and his impartial recording can lick a rock for all I care. Hm, let's think. Where are you from?"

Pesdari nearly said the Coven but remembered Cigma's warning just in time. Instead, she answered with, "Yrecep Forest."

The cantor broke out into a fit of laughter.

"No!" Nyfun wheezed, waving her hands about. "I appreciate the dramatic inclination, but it has to be *somewhat* realistic. Tell me where you're really from."

Pesdari stared blankly at her. Nyfun's mouth dropped.

"You're joking... You aren't joking! Oh, how wonderfully mysterious! Absolutely wonderful! I shall call you the... the, hmmm," Nyfun mused. The shine of inspiration in her hazel eyes would have put any jewel to shame.

"The Executioner of Yrecep Forest! Yes, yes that's what I shall call you!"

"Don't call me that."

"Well, it's too late now! I've already committed it to memory!"

Capar giggled as Pesdari's brow furrowed. She didn't like this cantor.

"And you, little one? What is your name?" Nyfun's smiled at Capar.

"Capar! And this is my brother Anicen!"

Anicen was so taken with the cantor that he didn't realize his stolen scarf had begun to slip down his face. Nyfun's smile morphed into a look of shock.

"Y-your face!" the canter exclaimed. Anicen hastily pulled the scarf back up as Pesdari pointed her hand at the canter, unsure yet which element to unleash, but certain she would eliminate this new threat to Anicen quickly. The cantor raised her hands in submission.

"Now, now! There's no need for that! I'm a cantor! The

more strange you are, the better my story becomes," she nervously chuckled, eyeing Pesdari. Pesdari glanced at Anicen. He reached out a hand and gently lowered her arm. The cantor sighed with relief.

"There! That's better. We're all friends here, aren't we, Capar?"

The little boy smiled up at her with stars in his eyes. The harp suddenly appeared in her hands, and Nyfun strummed a jaunty tune.

"So! Where are we off to? To where does your journey take you?"

"Back to our village!" Capar told her. Nyfun plucked at the strings again, thoughtfully.

"Ah, a tale of homecoming. Always a crowd-pleaser! And how did you two become so, ah, transfigured?"

"A horrible witch did this to us. Then Pesdari saved us!"

Pesdari ignored the cantor and turned to look over her shoulder.

"Come. We should leave here."

"Do you even know where you're going?" Nyfun asked serenely. "You are from... *Yrecep Forest* after all."

The cantor bore a smirk at the mention of the name. Pesdari glared at her.

"I'm sure you don't get out much. I'll be your guide! Free of charge!" the cantor continued.

"No. We'll find our own way."

"Oh, please, Pesdari! Let her come with us! Anicen and I have never been to the big town. We don't know the way home!"

"And you do know the way, cantor?" asked Pesdari suspiciously. Nyfun responded with a dramatic hand flourish and said, "But of course! There's a plains village just two days from here. That's where you come from isn't it, boys? I passed by it on my travels to this very town."

The boys began to cheer, yip, and dance at the thought of

going home.

"Fine," Pesdari scowled at Nyfun. "But you will do as I say."

Nyfun slapped a hand over her heart.

"My thanks to you, The Executioner of Yrecep Forest! It's the least I could do after saving you from the guards after all," she gushed. Anicen's lips curled in a dog smile as Pesdari's scowl somehow got even deeper.

"I said don't call me that."

"Capar, is she always this disagreeable?"

"Yes," the boy laughed. Nyfun pulled an exaggerated face of dismay.

"Oh, dear."

"No, I'm not!" Pesdari snapped. With that, the troupe began to make their way with Capar giggling and Anicen chortling in his strange dog way at Pesdari's irritation.

Chapter 18
The Village

The first day of their long walk to Anicen and Capar's village was uneventful, boring even, but the dark-skinned cantor entertained the boys with songs and stories, most of which led Pesdari to believe that the cantor was terrible at her profession. The boys, however, thought Nyfun was wonderful, and Capar happily shared their story with her despite Pesdari's best efforts to keep him from revealing too much about the Coven.

Brisk winds swept them along their path, and thankfully Nyfun had a satchel hidden under her voluminous robes that held some flatbread and hard cheese. That first night, they slept under the stars. Hissing, Pesdari's fingers glowed red as she cauterized her wound. The brothers huddled together too tired from the past few days to do anything but sleep. Admittedly, they were a bit cold, but the thought of seeing their home again warmed the boys' hearts. As the sun dipped low on the second day of their travels, the village rose into sight. The thatched roofs of the modest homes sparkled like gold in the dying sunlight. Nyfun and Pesdari exchanged a rare, understanding look between them as Capar, "We're home! We're home!"

Eyes wide, Anicen stared at the village he had visited in dreams so often during his captivity.

"It's still here! The Vuglar didn't destroy it!" he thought, elated, but then his fingers rose to his muzzle.

"I don't want them to see me. Not like this."

Pesdari yanked Capar back just before he took off running.

"Wait. You're an aberration. You can't just go running in there. It might not be safe."

"What? What d'yah mean?" Capar asked, looking at his brother with worry. Nyfun quickly placed a comforting hand on his and Anicen's shoulders.

"Not quite the wording I would have used, Pesdari! But I suppose that's why you're the Executioner, and I, the cantor."

Pesdari glowered at Nyfun.

"Stop calling me that!"

The cantor ignored her and reassured the boys, "I'll go into the village first and... prepare them for your arrival!"

Then she added with a sly smile, "You two wait here with the Executioner."

Nyfun dexterously ducked as a clod of dirt and grass went sailing by her head. After swatting dust off of her robes, the canter waved to the group and began making her way up the hill.

...

When Nyfun entered the village, she saw old folks sitting in their doorways chattering and weaving baskets from yellow grasses. She strummed a cheery tune on her harp and flashed her most endearing smile.

"Greetings, greetings to my elders! I am-"

"-*Yer* elders? I don't recognize yah 'tall. Ateyub, yah must have gotten around more than we thought!" cackled one old woman who wore her braids like a crown. The so-named Ateyub squinted at Nyfun from his place on the ground. His hands stopped weaving as he considered this.

"No, no, that one's not one o' mine, Resion, I'm sure of it."

"How can yah be so sure? Worse than a billy goat yah were."

"Ah, those were the days!"

Nyfun joined in the good-spirited chuckling and tried again with a bit more grandiosity in her voice.

"I am the cantor, Nyfun!" she declared with an intricate curtsy that was less of a simple dip in the knees and more like the first steps of a dance.

"And what do yah want, cantor Nyfun?" asked another old woman, who wore a blue shawl and never looked away from her basket. Nyfun straightened up.

"I came from town. While I was there, two young lads requested that I give their family news of their well-being."

"Two boys? What are yah saying? All our young are accounted fer," Resion chimed in, a note of amusement in her voice.

"They've been gone for nigh a year, so they tell me," Nyfun responded, carefully watching her audience. A hush fell over the group. The old folk cast wary glances at one another.

"Isew," Resion nearly whispered to the woman in the blue shawl. "Could it be?"

"What are these boys' names?" Isew asked, looking directly at the cantor now. Her amber eyes bore into Nyfun like a sword. Nyfun decided the best thing to do was to come right out with it.

"Young Anicen travels with his brother, Capar," she said simply.

Resion gasped, and Ateyub smacked a fist to his chest.

"Don't mock us, girl!" he cried.

"How do yah know those names!" another voice cried out. Isew stood and raised a hand to silence the growing pandemonium.

"Cantor, those boys were lost to Yrecep Forest. Yah couldn't have met them. Yah must be mistaken."

"I am not, my good lady," Nyfun said. "Anicen and Capar are alive and well."

Wood clattered to the ground. At the edge of the group, a

woman stood, stock-still. Isew quickly gestured for her to be led forward. Resion and Ateyub held the stricken woman by the elbows. She had gone as white as a bone.

"This might be nothing, Ethrom," Isew quickly said. Nyfun looked Ethrom over, something in her face was familiar.

"My boys," the woman breathed, glancing frantically between Isew and Nyfun.

"*She's their mother*," the cantor realized.

"Anicen and Capar want to come home, but I must speak with you," Nyfun said to Ethrom urgently.

"What? Why aren't they with yah?" Ethrom asked, beginning to look for her sons in the distance.

"Please, let us talk somewhere alone."

"Why? What'ev yah done with my sons!"

"Nothing! Nothing, woman! But I must speak with you!"

Isew's lined brow grew a few more wrinkles as she took Ethrom by the hands.

"Come. Come, we'll talk inside," she said, turning to enter her small abode. Nyfun followed and shut the door. The canter took a breath as Isew and Ethrom stared at her.

"Anicen and Capar are alive," she told them. Ethrom let out a wail and fell to her knees.

"Thank the gods! Oh, thank the gods!"

"Where are they?" Isew asked curtly. Nyfun held up a hand.

"First, I must tell you something. Your sons have been cursed."

Both Ethrom and Isew were too stunned for words. Nyfun began to tell the tale of the boys lost in Yrecep Forest.

"After you sent them to Yrecep Fores to hide, they were captured."

She continued to speak of the Coven and the horrible magic that had been performed on the two boys. Hearing of her sons' afflictions, Ethrom began to cry.

"But they are alive," Nyfun repeatedly firmly. "And they

want to come home if you'll receive them."

Ethrom looked at her with pain in her eyes.

"Anicen can't talk?"

"He communicates, but he cannot speak like you or I can."

Ethrom rubbed her face and stood. She resolutely walked to the door, turning over her shoulder to say, "I'll fetch Fearth. Bring me my sons. Bring them here."

Nyfun watched her go. Once Ethrom had left, she turned to Isew.

"Will the boys be safe here? Will the rest of the village accept them cursed as they are?"

Isew scowled at the canter for the thought. Nyfun pursed her own lips. She had been getting evil eyes quite a lot recently, and she was quite tired of it.

"Those boys belong with the village. We take care of our own here."

Nyfun nodded and began to make her exit. Before she left, she said, "One more travels with them. A great sorceress. She helped them escape."

Isew paused before she said, "Bring her as well. But tell her to keep her magic to herself. It's done enough harm."

...

Pesdari sat on the ground, massaging her sore feet. Her wounded leg ached, but she was more preoccupied with watching the boys nervously pace and twitch as they waited for the cantor to return. Anicen's stomach wriggled unhappily as he stared at the village on the hill. What were they saying up there? He had prayed to see his home again for so long, but now the thought of running up what hill filled him with dread.

"What will they think of my face?" he fretted. An involuntary whined crept through his lips. Capar bumped him with his shoulder.

"It'll be alright! Ma and Pa will want to see us," he said

earnestly. Anicen rubbed his feet in the dirt. Pesdari cast a sidelong glance at the pair.

"Don't be so certain. You two are aberrations. We might have to move on," she said. Capar's face screwed up into one of apprehension and anger as he yelled, "Stop saying that! I'm going home! I'm not an abe-aber... aberration!"

He angrily wiped away tears that began streaming down his face. Pesdari stood from her place on the ground and pointed at him.

"Be quiet. What is, must be. You can't change that. We'll move on if they won't have you."

Anicen cocked his head, pointing to Pesdari before gesturing toward himself and Capar. Pulling her mouth to one side, Pesdari looked away from him, but said, "Yes. I won't just abandon you two. How would you eat? You can barely start a fire on your own."

Nyfun, with all her splendid colors, appeared as suddenly as if she had sprung up out of the ground. Pesdari jumped and shrieked at the dramatic arrival much to Nyfun's amusement.

"They want to see you!" she exclaimed, a bit winded from running all the way down the hill. Anicen froze when a man's voice rang out.

"Anicen! Capar!"

They all turned towards the village. A tall, lean man was shouting and running down to them. A woman chased after him. Anicen pressed his hands to his eyes and began to cry. His parents were coming for him, just as they had promised so long ago.

"My sons!" Ethrom cried. In no time at all, the long heartbroken parents reached their children. Fearth clasped Capar close to him. Ethrom was wrestling with Anicen who had locked his arms around his face.

"Anicen! Anicen!" sobbed Ethrom. "Let me see yah, boy!"

Slowly, Anicen lowered his arms. The muscles in Ethrom's jaw clenched, but she pulled him to her chest.

"Oh, my boy. My dear, dear boy," she whispered in his hair. Fearth stared at his son's muzzle before looking Capar over.

Capar stared up at his father. The man had changed. A thick black beard sprouted from his chin and a patch covered his left eye. The developments left the young boy a little shaken.

"Yah look different, Pa, but I look a little different too now I suppose."

Capar pushed back his hood so his father could see him exactly as he was. Fearth's good eye widened.

"Horns. I didn't believe it," he breathed.

"They're good for headbutting," Capar said, quite matter of fact. Fearth scratched the skin above his eye patch nervously.

"Yah are right," he managed. "They are good for that."

Then Ethrom was grabbing at Capar and covering his face in kisses. Fearth went to Anicen. The boy stared at his father, too scared of what the man would think to move. His father inspected his shoulders, arms and legs looking for any injuries. Then, the man placed his big hands on Anicen's shoulders.

"Yah looked out for yer brother. Yah both came home. Honor to yah, boy."

Anicen's body was wracked with sobbing. Pesdari couldn't help the twitch in her lip. Half-human cries intermingled with a dog's howling. It was a sound that never should have existed. Anicen was a creature of Thade's twisted creation, but Fearth didn't seem to notice. Something in Pesdari ached as she watched the man hold his son tight and kiss the top of the boy's head.

"Yah are home.

Chapter 19

The Raid

Anicen and Capar's homecoming was both wonderful and strange. While all the villagers were happy to see the two returned home alive, Anicen knew their current appearances were shocking. Still, there had been an impromptu feast thrown in their honor. Three rough-hewn chairs were placed before a large bonfire, places of honor reserved for Anicen, Capar, and Pesdari.

Pesdari felt uncomfortable with all the eyes of the village on her, but the food was tasty and it felt good to give her aching leg a rest. Nyfun sang their story for the entire village. Some of her artistic flourishes in the tale, like the fact that Thade had a serpent's tongue and that Pesdari was the personification of justice, had her rolling her eyes, but she was begrudgingly impressed with Nyfun's attention to detail. As Nyfun's song came to a close, Isew stood and looked to Pesdari. "We thank the Executioner of Yrecep Forest for returning our lost children to us. We thank the gods for their mercy. Let us feast together. Remember that the circle is forever, but this joy may be for a moment!"

Isew held a wooden cup high into the air.

"To Anicen and Capar! To the Executioner of Yrecep Forest!"

The crowd joyously repeated the toast, and all drank and

were merry. When the fire began to die down, Fearth and Ethrom approached Pesdari.

"Please, stay in our home tonight. Our home isn't large, but we have a bed for yah."

Before Pesdari could speak, Isew interjected.

"Fearth and Ethrom, yah've just got the one bed. Spend this night with yer sons. I will house Pesdari tonight. Tomorrow night yah can host her."

A little chastened, Fearth and Ehtrom nodded, but as they turned to their sons, their faces brightened again. "Come on boys! To bed!" their father bellowed. Capar clutched at Fearth's arm, screaming with laughter as the man raised him into the air. Ehtrom rested her hand upon the back of Anicen's head as the family went home. As Pesdari walked with Isew, she turned her head to watch the family gather together with a sad smile. Surprising as the thought was, she would miss those boys Pesdari looked around then; these buildings still fascinated her. There was so much that was the same about her former home, and yet the two were nothing alike. Broad wood beams stretched overhead and dried flowers hung from them. Shelves on the wall held clay bottles among other assorted items. Wood walls surrounded her.

"It's like living in a tree," Pesdari smiled to herself. She liked the idea actually, like the thought of being able to take wing at a moment's notice as birds do. There had been enough traveling for her the past few days though. Tonight, she would rest.

...

Capar woke with a start as the door to their home slammed shut. He heard his mother whisper, "No, no! Not now!"

And then horrible words that made Capar's heart race rang through the air.

"The Vuglar are coming!"

His mother was kneeling before him saying something, but he couldn't hear her. She shook Anicen awake. Capar's throat seemed to close, and he began to shiver. He had heard those words before. Those words had launched his terrible journey into Yrecep Forest and led to his becoming, he touched his horns, like this. Anicen, awake now, was nodding as his mother spoke to him. Then, she was gone. Anicen looked at his brother with a close approximation of a smile. More villagers were shouting about the Vuglar now.

He tried to convey that everything would be alright to Capar, whose breath was beginning to slow as he comforted him. He ruffled his brother's hair before moving the younger boy under his parents' bed and then stuffed their blankets beneath the frame to hide him. Standing back, Anicen made sure that it looked like nothing more than old laundry was shoved under the bed. Then he ran to find his parents and Pesdari.

Outside, flaming arrows pierced thatched roofs and humans alike. Pesdari stood in the midst of the destruction, seething. She had left the Coven to escape death, not stumble into it every other day, and this enemy in particular had earned her hatred. The Vuglar. Her mother's dying breath echoed in her ears and feeling her father's pain as they had killed him burned in her memory. A burning arrow landed in the ground next to her feet. Her eyes went wild with violent delight, and she threw back her head to cackle.

She would show these fools the true power of fire. She hurried past a screaming woman whose shoulder was pierced through by one of the flaming projectiles. She growled. Her leg wouldn't allow her to run at full speed. Using her staff, she pushed herself forward. Isew was already grabbing the unfortunate, desperately trying to extinguish the flames before the woman was set alight. Pesdari dashed into Isew's abode and began snatching the clay bottles she had seen earlier. Anicen stood behind her in the doorway. She looked over her shoulder, her eyes cold.

"Give me your shirt!"

The boy handed it to her without hesitation. Immediately, she began tearing the garment to shreds, and then she began to concentrate. She wracked her brain for the precise movements and whispers Riefon had shared with her once. A cold grin spread across her face. She remembered how to trap fire in a bottle. Lip twitching with ill intent, she began to stuff the rags into the bottles, ten in all. She coaxed sparks to life within the bottles. Quickly, she handed five to Anicen. Then, with five gathered in one arm and her staff in her free hand, Pesdari stood.

"Follow me!" she ordered before she rushed out into the battle with Anicen on her heels. She clumsily began to descend the hill till she stood between the village and the raiding party. The Vuglar were still gathered at the bottom of the hill, letting their archers have their fun. They shouted with blood lust. Their steeds stomped and snorted. When Pesdari looked down upon them, she couldn't help but think of her brethren before a sacrifice was offered — bloodthirsty beasts eager for power and death.

"Burn, you wretches," she snarled. The scraps of cloth curled in the jars and burned even as she put the stoppers in. She could feel the heat through the clay. Then, she drew back her arm and threw. As the first jar launched through the air, Pesdari thought she heard the Vuglar laughing. She watched the jar strike at the feet of one of the mounts. The grass burst into flames. Anicen launched a second bottle. More fire erupted at the landing sites. The lumes bucked and kicked sending several of their riders into the flames. One of the raiding party blew into a horn, sending a bellowing cry into the air.

The Vuglar charged. As they raced up the hill, some narrowly avoided the missiles Pesdari and Anicen continued to throw. Raiders toppled left and right as the pair threw their deadly missiles. One Vuglar raider had made it through the bombardment and her steed was rapidly gaining ground. Pesdari was out of ammunition but by no means helpless. She gripped her staff with two hands and shoved at the legs of the approaching lume, sending both beast and rider to the ground. Pointing the staff at the raider, Pesdari smiled like a person possessed. Dirt encapsulated the furious raider who struggled against her earthen prison, but it was no use. With a final gargled cry, the raider disappeared below the ground. Pesdari was taken aback and looked at her staff. Immediately, it began to vibrate in her grasp.

To her left, Anicen was doing battle with another raider. Anicen's jaws had clamped down on the raider's sword arm. He shook his head to and fro, ripping and tearing at the skin. As the sword dropped, he released his bite and snapped at the raider's throat. Screaming, the raider kicked the boy and turned to run. Pesari pointed the staff at the ground as another group of raiders rushed her. The ground erupted, sending the raiders flying into the air. They landed with a sickening crunch.

Suddenly a sword was slashing through the air at Pesdari. She threw herself out of its path, barely maintaining control of her staff. The Vuglar raider swung his sword again. He dismounted and moved with ease through the tall grass. Pesdari thrust her staff into the air and twisted it. A tornado materialized in front of her, directly on the raider. As the man was tossed like a rag doll through the air, Pesdari stared in wonder at her staff.

"This... this has been so easy," she thought. She never would have been able to exert such control and with such ease before. She was only a little tired. If anything, she felt exhilarated. The remaining raiders seeing their compatriot treated like a leaf on the wind, screamed for a retreat. Shocked and frightened, the Vuglar ran from the village. As the raiding party rode off, Nyfun emerged on the crest of the hill.

"Run! Run you cowards from the Executioner of Yrecep Forest!" she cried out. Strumming her harp, the cantor sang,

"No need for gallows or the axe! The Executioner of Yrecep Forest will blow ye to ash! Reifon himself trapped in a bottle. Beware the Executioner who gives even the gods a throttle!"

Anicen and Pesdari were surrounded by a group of villagers now who lifted the pair into the air.

"Hail to the Executioner of Yrecep Forest! Hail! Hail to Anicen! Protector of the village!" cheered the villagers. Anicen barked a laugh at Pesdari's bewildered face. The villagers carried them back to the smoldering village. Anicen could see his mother on the roof of one of the burning homes, beating at the flames with a blanket. Wiping her sweaty brow, Ethrom looked out and squinted. Was that smoke coming from Yrecep Forest? Surely not, the woman reasoned. Smoke from the burning homes must have drifted over to the black trees. But Ethrom was wrong. Yrecep Forest was indeed burning.

Chapter 20

The Fire

"Something's happening in Yrecep Forest!" a villager cried out. Isew drew in a sharp breath as she looked toward the accursed place.

"What new terror is this," she muttered. Then she called out to the rest of the village, "Focus on our own burnt homes! Yer injured kinfolk! Later we'll worry about the forest."

And so for three days, the villagers repaired their homes, tended to their wounds, and buried their dead — of which there were little thanks to Pesadri driving off the Vuglar. Although they tried to not discuss it, none could help casting their eyes to the dark plumes of smoke that rose from the forest, and all began to fret as the destruction seemed to draw closer and closer.

"What is coming?" the villagers whispered to each other. On the third day, Pesdari heard the whispers, and she told them exactly what was approaching through the forest.

"A friend," Pesdari replied, darkly. The villagers exchanged confused, frightened looks.

"A friend? What sort of friend comes bearing fire like that?"

"One of mine. And she means to kill me."

This sent gasps through the crowd

"What have yah brought here?" the villagers demand to

know.

"Tell yer *friend* to leave us be!"

"Take yer dark magic and go before it gets us all killed," shouted another. Suddenly, Isew was among them, glowering at the anxious crow.

"Yah fools! She brought our children home! She brought us victory!" Isew chides the crowd. "We have no reason not to trust her. We owe her our lives!"

"But Isew-"

"Be about yer business, I tell you! Whatever it is that comes, the Executioner of Yrecep Forest will deal with it. Isn't that right?" she asked Pesdari, leaving no room for quarter. Taken aback, Pesdari answered, "Y-yes. I will deal with it."

Isew nodded and waved her hands at the crowd. "Now get! Get!" As the crowd dispersed, Isew gripped Pesdari's arm and walked her toward the slope of the hill that led to Yrecep Forest.

"It's a good thing yer going to deal with this *friend*, as it looks like she's here."

Pesdari sucked air through her teeth as she saw flames charging through the black trees.

...

In the forest, shadows swirled around Thade. She shrieked and screamed with hideous laughter as the Dowhas tried to stop her onslaught. Flames erupted from every part of her — her hair, her eyes, her hands. Her body burned with ecstasy and so too did the Dowhas burn. Crackling black trees fell around her. Nightmare tried to swallow her in darkness, but with a delirious grin, Thade burst into a sun. With a wordless scream, the shadowy creature evaporated into nothing. She was at the edge of the forest now, and she could see someone coming down a hill toward her. With a delighted gasp, Thade recognized the figure. It was Pesdari!

Pesdari came closer to the trees and could see but an outline of her former friend. One last Dowhas remained, Tibarb. Her father's shadowy form clutched and tore at the wrathful young woman. Pesdari's guts went cold with dread. She began to run, her wounded leg causing her to stumble.

"Let her go! Leave it! She'll destroy you!" she cried out, but whatever remained of her father within that shadow would not let go. He pulled as hard as he could, and every so often Thade's face would be covered in shadow, but her flames always burned away the creeping darkness.

Both young women were releasing their war cries now. Thade dragged the shadow behind her, determined to kill. Pesdari rushed forward, her heart bursting. Just as Thade stomped out of the threshold of the trees, she arched back with a mighty cry. Blue flames spiked out of her spine and thrust themselves deep into Tibarb's being.

"No! No! No!" Pesdari screamed, watching the shadow dissolve into nothing. Thade's flames rescinded as she panted heavily. Pesdari stood in shocked silence.

"You..." she started. "You killed him."

Thade laughed again. She was brimming with so much power she was giddy. "You were going to kill me! But you're upset over a shadow? I'll give you something to be truly upset over!"

With a gust of wind, Thade launched herself at Pesdari. Her hands of fire swiped at Pesdari, who held her staff up with two hands to defend herself. The heat was overwhelming and not a cloud floated in the sky. Pesari had no ready water source to douse Thade's flames or drown the woman who had once been her only friend. Sneering, Thade raised a foot and slammed it down on Pesdari's right knee. With a cry, she tried to get back to her feet, but her leg was searing with pain. Thade's smile was cruel as she stared at her wounded foe.

"All I wanted was for us to live forever. And you tried to kill me. Why? Because I turned on our ways? You hated the

Coven."

Pesdari's laugh was short and sharp.

"I tried to kill you for food and a way out of the caves."

Thade's eyes widened in disbelief. Her mouth gaped before a roar of true resentment ripped through her. She vaulted herself at Pesdari and tried to claw at her throat, her eyes — at any flesh she could get her nails into. Allowing Thade to tear at her cheeks, Pesari thrust her fingers into the dirt as Thade began to blaze. Shifting at her command, the earth danced with relish. The blazing woman tilted, off-kilter. Quickly, Pesdari shoved her off. She wiped the blood from her cheeks onto her hands and spit into her palms. Diving she grasped the dirt near Thade's ankles and closed her eyes. She rolled away as the ground bubbled and squelched. Thade tried to move and screamed with fury, realizing that her legs below the knee were trapped in the newly formed mud.

"Pest! Pest!" she cried out. Pesdari limped over to her staff and picked it up. Snarling, Thade's eyes glowed red. Just as Thade raised her hands to shoot her desired target full of fire, Pesdari threw the staff into Thade's chest. The staff turned white with heat. Erupting flames engulfed Thade, and a sudden funnel of wind swept the flames higher. Pesdari stared as fire of her own design devoured Thade at her very core. In the brilliant light, Pesdari saw Riefon appear. The skeleton wrapped his arms around Thade's torso, whispering in the roaring flames, "It is finished, little ember. Rest. The circle closes."

Thade's skin began to simmer, turning black with the ferocity of the flames. She did not surrender quietly. She bucked, screamed, and tore at her own burning skin, but the ancient god clutched her close. Pesdari watched the life leave Thades's eyes and saw the childhood friend she had betrayed. A charred corpse collapsed to the ground before the Executioner of Yrecep Forest. She stared down at it. In the smoke above, hovered Riefon like a dark cloud. The air was eerily quiet.

"How do I heal the boys?" Pesdari asked, breaking the silence. Riefon cracked out a horrible laugh.

"You must hurt them to heal them, of course. Cleanse them with fire. Make them right within this world."

Tapping the tip of his skeletal finger against Pesdari's forehead, her mind was seared with images of how to complete her task. With that final message, the god disappeared as ash on the wind. Pesdari slowly limped her way back to the throng of villagers that stood waiting for her, jubilant as well as anxious.

"You have nothing to fear now," she told them, tired and eyes dull. As she walked, she turned her head to Isew. "Bring me bandages. And whatever healing herbs you have."

"Are yah hurt?" the old woman asked.

Ignoring her, Pesdari repeated her request. Without a second thought, Isew hurried to her home for the requested items. A few minutes later, Pesdari and Isew stood outside Anicen's home. They walked inside. Ehtrom and Fearth stared, dismayed by the bloody sight of her. With no energy for pleasantries, Pesdari was blunt.

"I can heal your sons."

"How?!" Ethrom gasped. Pesdari shook her head.

"It's best you not know. Leave me with Anicen for now."

Anicen looked at his mother, a bit frightened, but she held his hand and whispered, "It'll be alright! She'll help yah!"

Fearth stared at Pesdari, concerned, but at his wife's urging he took Capar, and the three of them left the room. Anicen sat on the edge of the bed watching Pesdari take one of his mother's waterskins off the wall and fill a bowl with water.

Then, she crumbled the herbs Isew had gathered into the bowl and soaked the rags in the concoction. Pesdari picked at the scratches on her cheeks till fresh blood flowed. Once her fingers were coated with blood, she dipped them into the bowl.

"I must hurt you to heal you," she said, swirling the mixture to be sure all the ingredients intermingled properly.

Anicen cocked his head, confused. With an apologetic smile, Pesdari stood and cradled Anicen's head with her left hand. Her right palm pressed against his muzzle. Then, her hand blazed white with heat. Anicen's eyes rolled back in his head. The room was filled with the smell of burning flesh and fur.

"Quickly! The bandages!" Pesdari called out as she withdrew her hand from the bloody and tortured boy. Horrified, Isew stared at Anicen's burnt face.

"Now!"

Isew rushed to her task, wrapping the boy up in the soaking bandages. Anicen, thankfully, had passed out during the spell, so he felt nothing as the two wrapped his wounded flesh. Their task completed, Isew placed her hand gently on Pesdari's elbow.

"You are welcome here. You've saved us from two terrors. There's no need for you to leave. Call this place your home."

Pesdari stared at her, almost too bewildered to comprehend what she was saying. She held up her bloody hands and quietly began to speak, "My kin are all dead. I've killed the only friend I ever had. I shouldn't stay here."

Isew wet a fresh rag. She started cleaning Pesdari's face and hands.

"Yah gave yer blood for this village. That makes yah our blood, and we don't cast out blood."

The two sat silently as tears rolled won Pesdari's cheeks, and Isew continued to tend to her.

...

"When will he wake up?" Capar whined to his father as they started on a new chore together. It had been two days since Pesdari had done whatever it was she said would fix Anicen, and he was on strict orders not to bother either of them as they recuperated. He really wanted to see Anicen. He wondered what Pesdari had done to his brother. His pa had said that Anicen was sleeping, but who slept for two days straight? When he had tried to see Pesdari at Isew's home, the woman had run him off, telling him that she was not to be disturbed. Absently, Capar touched his horns. He really hoped that Pesdari wouldn't take them away when she was feeling better. He was starting to like them. His father wiped at his brow and flicked a little rock off his son's horns.

"Pesdari said to give it time," Fearth said calmly, not wanting to admit that he was anxious for his oldest son's recovery.

Inside their family home, a sound disturbed the sleeping Ethrom. She rubbed her eyes, murmuring "Anicen? Are yah finally awake?"

Sitting up, Anicen looked at his mother and smiled.

"I'm awake, Ma."

The End

www.ingramcontent.com/pod-product-compliance
Lightning Source LLC
Chambersburg PA
CBHW061103100726
47911CB00012B/375